UPWARD BOUND

UPWARD BOUND

WOODY BROWN

JONATHAN CAPE
LONDON

1 3 5 7 9 10 8 6 4 2

Jonathan Cape, an imprint of Vintage, is part of
the Penguin Random House group of companies

Vintage, Penguin Random House UK,
One Embassy Gardens, 8 Viaduct Gardens, London SW11 7BW

penguin.co.uk/vintage
global.penguinrandomhouse.com

First published in Great Britain by Jonathan Cape in 2026
First published in the United States of America by Hogarth, an imprint of
Random House, a division of Penguin Random House LLC in 2026

Copyright © Woody Brown 2026

The moral right of the author has been asserted

This novel is a work of fiction. Although it is loosely inspired by certain experiences
in the author's life, the story, characters and events depicted herein are fictional creations.
It is not intended to be a factual portrayal or account of any specific person or occurrence.

Penguin Random House values and supports copyright. Copyright fuels creativity,
encourages diverse voices, promotes freedom of expression and supports a vibrant culture.
Thank you for purchasing an authorised edition of this book and for respecting intellectual
property laws by not reproducing, scanning or distributing any part of it by any means
without permission. You are supporting authors and enabling Penguin Random House to
continue to publish books for everyone. No part of this book may be used or reproduced
in any manner for the purpose of training artificial intelligence technologies or systems.
In accordance with Article 4(3) of the DSM Directive 2019/790, Penguin Random House
expressly reserves this work from the text and data mining exception.

Printed and bound in Great Britain by Clays Ltd, Elcograf S.p.A.

The authorised representative in the EEA is Penguin Random House Ireland,
Morrison Chambers, 32 Nassau Street, Dublin D02 YH68

A CIP catalogue record for this book is available from the British Library

ISBN 9781787336414

Penguin Random House is committed to a sustainable future
for our business, our readers and our planet. This book is
made from Forest Stewardship Council® certified paper.

To Mary,
the giver of all good things,

and Drew,
who loves me best of all

You have caused confusion and delay.
—SIR TOPHAM HATT, *Thomas & Friends*

Little engines CAN do big things.
—THOMAS THE TANK ENGINE

UPWARD BOUND

THE ELOPER

The best I could come up with was, "Thomas has left the station."

I was sitting in the rec room, waiting to be told what to do next, when I saw Jorge slip out via the back door that leads to the pool and the parking lot. There were probably a dozen of us inmates in the rec room. A few staffers were there, but they were huddled in a group, talking with great animation about an episode of *Love Island*. Mom wouldn't watch that show so I hadn't seen it, either. Sounds contentious but also sexy. If Carlos had been there, he'd have told them to get back to work, but he'd have said it in a cool way that wouldn't make anyone resentful. The staffers obviously felt no urgency to set up our next activity. You could tell that it didn't even occur to them that we might mind being left waiting. As if time means nothing to people who have nothing but time. I think it's the opposite. Our time is wasted so profligately that we cherish it for what it might be, not for its emptiness.

I doubted seriously that Jorge was really plotting to escape or to take an unauthorized swim, but he is utter stealth itself when in elope mode. Still, I wanted someone to know that he'd left the building. I went through my available scripts to find a Thomas or *Toy Story* phrase that I could utter that would function in this situation. For reasons I can't explain, I am not able to summon a timely, unique message that I can say with my mouth. I can, however, repeat a phrase from an often-viewed video. They call this "echolalia" for what it's worth. In this particular moment, the best I could come up with was:

"Thomas has left the station."

I am the echolalic guy who cried wolf too many times, so naturally, no one paid the slightest attention. My mom is the only one capable of translating my echolalic scripts into functional communication. Everyone else assumes my phrases are nonsense. The staffers didn't even look in my direction, and the other inmates have been trained to be useless. I sat for a moment, but then I lumbered to my feet. It took heavy concentration and motor planning to propel my awkward body in the direction Jorge had gone. My idea was to double the chance that someone would notice a client was missing. I had no personal reason to flee. My top priorities are familiarity and routine, and this action provided neither. But I also didn't want anything to happen to Jorge.

I went through the door that opened into a corner of the parking lot. The pool was to my right, but it was gated and locked. I couldn't see Jorge anywhere. The car entrance gate was open for the cars, so I walked in that direction to see if he had gone off the property. I looked up and down the street. I hoped he hadn't crossed over to the park. I didn't want to risk my own life dodging traffic. No sight of Jorge. Then I glanced over to the little grassy area tucked away on the other side of the parking lot. There were a couple of play apparatuses there, and it was shady. I walked over there. I could see Jorge's big feet sticking out of the terra-cotta tunnel. I knew that spot. It's cool and quiet in there. I had no need to disturb him now that I had found him and knew he was safe. I would just wait for someone to come along. There was a bench next to the basketball hoop. I sat down. I counted cars that passed. There weren't many.

*

I've spent plenty of time with Jorge. I probably understand his predicament better than the people whose job it is to handle him. Jorge and I are both inmates at an insane asylum that passes itself off as a day program for autistic young adults. We have been in and out of each other's lives since special ed preschool. We graduated from different schools—well, I graduated. He got a certificate of completion. But there is only one place in this city for people like us to go after high school, so here we are. Reunited.

Jorge and I have shared space off and on for nearly twenty years, but we have never had anything that resembles a conversation. That probably seems incredible, but it's standard for nonspeakers. Jorge has an admirable level of acceptance about his situation. He doesn't seem consumed by the frustration, anxiety, and anger that tortures many people who lack speech. Some of us are like tightly wound tops. With a flick of a wrist, we can spin and skitter out of control. Not Jorge. He falls into the category of gentle giant. The first thing you notice about him is his immense size. He is tall, but he's almost as big around as he is up and down. He usually slumps and hangs his head, as if the act of being big ol' Jorge is a weighty burden. He is the least aggressive inmate—I should say client—in this sad, boring place. He's too big to move with any conscious belligerence, and he's too gentle to get riled in the first place. Jorge presents only one behavioral challenge at Upward Bound, which is probably the most cynical name they could have given this dead-end way station. Jorge is what they call an eloper. If you look away for an instant, Jorge is gone. He moves like a specter when no eyeballs are trained on him. This isn't a problem most of the time; the adult babysitters keep the doors locked in this place. But when we go on our weekly field trips to Target, a staffer is assigned specifically to Jorge. Thankfully, I don't require this level of supervision.

People can be elitist when it comes to speech. If you can't communicate, it must mean that you are mentally retarded. In the special ed room, math consisted of learning how to make change, and English meant picture books. Unlike Jorge, I had a ticket out. My parents refused to accept that I was an idiot. They saw this Indian lady on *60 Minutes* who had taught her nonspeaking son to type and they tracked her down. I was three when I met Soma. She showed me how to point and make choices of words and letters. By the time I started school, I could spell and do simple math better than my neurotypical peers. The catch was that I needed an aide beside me to hold up the little laminated board with a QWERTY alphabet and basic punctuation marks on it. The aide needed to be trained to help me stay on task.

Autism on my end of the spectrum is like ADHD times a thousand. It's nearly impossible for me to untangle the many channels in my brain so that I can stay on a single station. It's like sitting in front of a bank of monitors that are all showing different events, and all are playing at top volume. The aide uses prompts, repeating the letter or word I've just pointed to, to keep me on track so that I can complete a thought. My brain can easily switch to another channel and the communication drifts away unfinished. The aide shakes the letter board when I get derailed to regain my attention. The sustaining of my attention is a dance of subtle cues and prompts. It's not a dance you learn on the first try. Training can take a while, but it's crucial. It's also important that the aide has a core of calm. I pick up on the energy. My focus is obliterated if the person helping me is stressed or lacks confidence. Good soul + good training = good aide. A tall order for a low-paying gig.

The public school had no idea what to do with me. My mom tried to show them, offered to train an aide, just as she had been trained by Soma. School administrators said no. I kept going to school, bored and chagrined in special ed. Mom had to work, but she worked from home as a technical writer. If you have a kid like me, you have to be flexible. Mom spent several hours after school giving me little lessons in math, science, and history. She made the school give her the textbooks that the typical kids worked from. She read to me every day from children's classics and poetry. She kept me at grade level. I have to confess that my behavior during this period was challenging to say the least. I was not submitting quietly to instruction. The special ed teacher and the school psychologist might presume that I didn't want to learn. My mom forged ahead anyway. I don't know which came first: my desire to learn or her passion for me to get a proper education. At any rate, I was finally allowed to sit in the corner of the remedial class, where I worked with my aide one-on-one. It felt like my life had finally begun the day the teacher invited me to join the remedial learners in a group lesson. Thanks to my mom's sessions at home, I was already ahead of the other students. I didn't mind. It gave me the bandwidth I needed to work on controlling my autistic behaviors in class.

By high school, I was on diploma track. This constituted a minor miracle. Most of the severely autistic kids I started out with had been quietly shunted off to special schools where they couldn't bother anyone but each other. Jorge was bused to some place an hour away. None of us were expected to meet graduation requirements. My pointing and typing gave me entrée to a different outcome. I often wondered why the school district didn't try to replicate what I was doing with the others, like Jorge. I guess it was just too perplexing, or too much work. Or they had no warrior mom to force them into educating the losers they assumed to be ineducable.

I had another advantage. I had an aide who stuck with me through middle and high school. School aides usually come and go. Sal was a big friendly teddy bear who excelled at being my protector. The social anxiety of being a nonspeaking oddball at a big public high school was intense. Sal was like a comfort item who never got annoyed with me and always had my back. He may never have attained greatness as an aide with the letter board. He didn't have the fluency of the dance that Soma and my mom did, but he kept me calm and in the room. His face was so full of joy the night I crossed the high school stage and accepted my diploma. The accomplishment was his as much as mine. You should have seen my mom that night. She was weeping so hard she could barely speak.

But what next? The supports fall off after high school, like training wheels that I still needed to stay upright and moving forward. My parents refused to give in to the inevitability of Upward Bound. But college seemed like a nonstarter. How could I sit through a long lecture without making my weird noises? How could I even get into college with my spotty academic record? They don't let you have a communication partner to take the SATs. My mom had a realization. All you need to go to community college is a high school diploma, and I had one of those. I applied online and never had to mention my disability. Mom tried to hire and train an aide to go with me, but the first two quit. It was also incredibly expensive. There is public funding for caregivers who babysit, but not for academic support. Mom decided it would be easier to do it herself. She and my dad agreed that she would quit her job and she would be my aide at community college. It was an experiment.

I started with just one academic class. English 1A. Mom and I walked into the run-down old classroom. I made a beeline for a seat in the back row, farthest corner. I chose that so I would be less inclined to leave for an unscheduled break. The professor talked about herself and the books we'd be reading. She had everyone make a brief introduction. Mom held the letter board so that I could say it in my own words, which she read out loud. I thought we'd come across like a freak show, but no one batted an eye. Many students in the class had obstacles they had faced to be there. I wasn't the only outlier; it was a room full of outliers. The ninety-minute class flew by. It never occurred to me to take a break. Mom and I drove to campus for class every day, but I didn't hang out or study there—it was too chaotic for me. At home we worked on a strict schedule of reading and writing. Half hour of work, half hour of break, starting at eight A.M. and ending at five P.M. Dad, who worked from home, too, would stick his head in the door throughout the day, just to get some attention. Mom would pretend to be aggravated by the disruption, but being annoying was Dad's shtick. I enjoyed their banter. After five, my brain needed the calming effects of my video screens, dinner, and an early bedtime routine, which Dad oversaw.

The first real test was the midterm paper. I was never asked to write one in high school. As much as I wish I could just type my thoughts independently, that's not how it works for most nonspeaking spellers. Our brains have trouble getting all the motor planning lined up to perform the complex actions involved in typed communication. Most people don't consider how many parts of the brain are activated when they speak or type. If your electronic impulses resist firing in the right order, like mine and probably Jorge's do, the message gets lost somewhere between the thought and the finger hitting the keyboard. I needed Sal in high school for many reasons, but he lacked the structural organization to assist me in longer assignments like papers. Mom figured things out as she went. First she elicited from me a topic. I typed, "Assuming intelligence." The process involved in producing those two words took one half-hour session. Mom gave me a series of choices that distilled into my chosen subject matter. The next day she had me type out a thesis, then supporting ideas that became an outline. In thirty-minute increments daily over several weeks, I wrote a paper. I fashioned every idea and wrote every word, although I could not have executed any of it without Mom holding the board and keeping my brain on track.

"Okay, you've said you want to write about assuming intelligence. What are you thinking of for a thesis?" she said.

My fingers hopped across my letter board. She repeated the

words as I typed them, then repeated them again as she typed them into the computer when I finished a phrase or sentence. The repetition maintained my focus and momentum.

"Many. autistic. students. do. not. at. first. glance. appear. to. be. capable. of. sophisticated. thought." She answered my words twice as my fingers danced across the little board. Yes, I could have typed directly onto the computer keyboard myself. But my shaky fine-motor skills make my fingers detour to neighboring letters. I would spend more time fixing typos than writing. The simple, low-tech, laminated letter board that we made from a computer printout is forgiving if my finger goes a little off the mark.

That first paper got an A. What the hell. I kept challenging myself. I went from taking one class per semester to two, then three. I kept getting A's. I took all the general ed classes I needed to get my Associate of Arts degree and transfer to university. I could see a path in front of me.

Jorge, on the other hand, was taken out of his public school by the district when he was in the fifth grade. They sent him to a nonpublic school that catered specifically to autistic students. Everyone felt good about sending Jorge and the others to a specialized school. My mom toured it around that time. She was always on the lookout for a place where academics were a priority, where she didn't have to work so hard to convince people that I could learn the regular stuff. She came back annoyed. It was no better than the dummy special ed class at my current school. Some of her autism mom friends liked it just fine and sent their kids there. The problem was that a school like that didn't prepare autistic kids for anything except a lifetime at Upward Bound or its equivalent. The more regulated among us might look forward to a career as a box boy or a busboy, but the nonspeakers can't even do those menial jobs. An education might expose areas of strength that could lead to a more productive life. For Jorge and most of the others I grew up with, their dependence would be lifelong.

The bottom line is being able to communicate. I wonder if Jorge could have learned in school if an iPad and a trained aide had been available to him. You can see how helpful some alternative communication would have been. *Hey, Jorge! Why do you keep running off? What can we do to keep you in your prescribed location?* If Jorge could point and type like me, we could get to the bottom of this dangerous mystery. Unfortunately for him, there are very few aides trained in alternative communication. There are none at Upward Bound. Here, without a real communication partner, I am as mute as Jorge. Even if I knew with certainty why Jorge wanders away and what our minders could do to keep him safe, I would have no means by which to tell them.

*

Upward Bound is located in a shabby one-story building that used to be a nursing home. It still looks like one, with its eighties-era aqua-and-peach exterior and convenient ramp. The inmates have to sign in at the front desk when they arrive in the morning, or someone does it for them. I am capable of signing my name, but it takes me forever and looks like a kindergartner's scrawl, so I let my mom do it. There are various rooms, patios, and a dinky, kidney-shaped pool surrounded by cracked concrete in the back. Most of the action (a term that applies very loosely) takes place in a large rec room in the center. Picture a nursing home rec room that hasn't been updated since the first Bush administration. Old-school linoleum, accordion dividers, metal folding chairs, cheesy decorations hung for whatever holiday just passed. They feed us breakfast, which usually consists of generic sugary cereal in a Styrofoam bowl. The schedule for the day is scribbled on a big whiteboard in hourly increments. It is one infantilizing activity after another. An hour of gluing macaroni to popsicle sticks to make a picture frame. An hour of a "cooking" activity during which we make Chex Mix, combining processed salty and sweet bits in one big bowl, which we eat for snack. Lunch (even less nutritious than breakfast or snack) is followed by games like Cootie or Connect 4, maybe a swim if it's warm. The time in the pool doesn't suck, but still, one day feels like forever.

There might be a walk across the street to the park, where we big-ass adults sit on swings or meander about. I used to like going to a park (not this one, a nicer one) even when I was too big for a playground. Mom let me bring a backpack full of Thomas trains. I would meticulously line them up according to their standing on the Isle of Sodor. Thomas, Percy, James, and Henry always first. I would also use this opportunity to gaze peripherally at the typical kids at play. I could imagine I was one of them. But the Upward Bound walks to the park offer none of these pleasures. Their only purpose is to use up that particular segment of the day. Dave can brag that he got his clients outside. There aren't any activities planned. Were awkward grown people supposed to play Duck Duck Goose? Staffers casually surround the playground to keep elopers like Jorge contained. This makes them seem more like prison guards than helpful friends, and they pay more attention to each other than to us.

I can understand the impulse to flee. God knows I feel like dashing out screaming from this place a million times a day. But I have more self-control than that and am able to play the model inmate. Still, I don't get much intellectual stimulation here, so I've put some effort into forming theories about Jorge's dilemma. The most likely one is that Jorge isn't running away from anything. Jorge doesn't mean to escape. He is going *to* something. There is something somewhere else that he wants to see or do. He can't express his need, so he just goes. The staffers have never even noticed that every time Jorge has eluded them in Target, they find him in the toy section looking at Mr. Potato Head. I have no idea what the spud's appeal is to Jorge. The compulsion is so strong that you can see Jorge's brain visibly thrumming as soon as our clown car pulls into the Target parking lot. If I could, I would tell the staffers to make the toy section our first stop and give poor Jorge his Potato Head time before his own head explodes and he runs away.

Jorge, the other inmates, and I were just marking time at Upward Bound under the not-very-watchful eyes of the young, underpaid staffers. I was older than most of them. Many were from the nearby community college (two were my former classmates). Some were full-time if they couldn't find a better job. Some tried to engage; some were bored and snuck their phones out of their pockets when the supervisor was out of the room. If I could speak, I might have snitched on them. Sometimes there would be a staffer who took a shine to you and would hang out with you in particular. I attracted a few fans due to my intriguing, tragic circumstances, but turnover is high in crappy jobs like this, and none of my staffer pals lasted very long.

Darla is in law school now. She flirted with me in the way a smart, well-intended girl tries to make the autistic guy feel like he could actually have a girlfriend someday. It wasn't real, but attention from a pretty girl made the time go by faster. She knew I had gone to community college. She had gone there, too, and said she remembered seeing me on campus. I realize that I was memorable for looking weird and having my mother at my elbow. Still, I was flattered. I'm pretty sure she thought I was there as part of some autism program. I wanted so badly to tell her that I was a straight-up student with straight A's. I bet she would have appreciated that I was an English major and that I dreamed of supporting myself as a novelist. I would have told her that I wouldn't have minded working at a menial job, but my body is so disorganized that I would wander around aimlessly without someone to steer me in the right direction. I would have told her all that if my letter board hadn't been lying fallow at home, as useless as my AA diploma. But all I could do was try to keep my behaviors under control when she was near.

Even vocational programs for autistic adults refused to take me on. Becoming a novelist was a long shot, but the alternative was day care. Surely something would happen to prevent that.

Something did happen. My dad, the funniest, most loving person in the world, had a heart attack and died right after my community college graduation. Many people are loving and kind, but Dad was loving and needy and edgy. His quick temper had to do with his sensitivity to criticism. My mom would ask an innocent question about a domestic matter and he would hear an accusation in it. I never criticized him because I couldn't speak, and he didn't use the letter board with me. As a result of this, he loved me unconditionally. He showered me with affection. He took me to the movies every Saturday and helped me bathe every night. It's amazing to be loved the way he loved me. He adored my mom, too, although she was occasionally the target of his harsh reaction to a perceived insult. They were otherwise like perennial newlyweds, always hugging and kissing and laughing at each other's jokes.

Dad's heart attack shouldn't have come as a big surprise. Exercise and a healthy diet were not on his list of priorities. I have inherited his indolence and bad eating habits. Still, his death was so shocking that my mom and I were completely paralyzed for a couple of months. My little family had been a three-legged stool. Missing a leg meant that we tottered and fell.

Mom and I met with the lawyer and accountant. There was life insurance and whatnot, but it wasn't going to be enough to take care of us forever. I would've loved to have gotten an actual job, but the door to the working world was bolted from the inside. Mom realized that she would have to go back to work. She couldn't get her old job back, but she got hired as an administrative assistant at a big hospital.

I'm not able to go unsupervised, despite my age and intellect. There are several reasons for this. For one thing, I can't call 911. If there were an emergency, if I accidentally set a kitchen fire, I would be unable to initiate a phone call. I can perform routine tasks that I've done a million times, but the novel event paralyzes my body. Here's a far more likely scenario: I have this tendency to vocalize along with my videos. The more stressed I am, the more likely I am to play stressy clips, like the incinerator scene from *Toy Story 3*. My voice can get alarmingly high and shrieky. If it gets to be too much, Mom will come tell me to tone it down. If I were alone, there would be no checks on my behavior. Suppose a neighbor called the police because they heard screaming, as if someone were descending inexorably toward a fiery hellhole. Disturbing, no argument. Cop comes to the door. I would not be able to identify myself or answer the officer's questions. I would end up in a psych ward, or worse. No joke. It has happened to other nonspeakers we know. There are plenty of stories of people like me being mishandled in interactions with authorities.

So we were forced to stick me at Upward Bound for my safety. We insisted to each other that it was temporary, that Mom would find a better place for me, where nonspeakers were respected and their communication was facilitated.

No utopia has presented itself. Adult day care is adult day care.

*

Darla made my first few weeks at Upward Bound more bearable. Unfortunately, she left for law school. I didn't blame her. Staffers here have to put up with some tough stuff. Darla's duties included changing diapers, cleaning poop and vomit, and dealing with meltdowns. Some of which may have been mine. It's one thing when the population is tiny kids, but when the soiled underpants belong to a severely autistic adult, many staffers decide that working at McDonald's would be less of a hassle. I can only imagine that working here would make law school look like fun. I almost got it together to hug Darla on her last day, but my body chose instead to flee the scene. I'm hoping that Darla realized how much I appreciated her attention. I hope she remembers me a little.

Jorge was luckier than me. He developed a bond with a guy named Carlos, who was a little older than the average zookeeper. Carlos was as thin and wiry as Jorge was large and floppy. They gave off a copacetic vibe. Both were undemanding and never cranky. Carlos was surprisingly competent in a quiet way that could go unnoticed. Jorge was quietly complacent and also overlooked. They would naturally seek each other out in the group and sit together like a couple of satisfied buddhas. If there was a small-group activity, like playing Hungry Hungry Hippos or making puppets out of paper bags, Carlos always kept Jorge in his section. Unlike Darla, who was on her way somewhere else, Carlos seemed like a lifer. He looked as if he actually enjoyed the work. He didn't have his heart set on some other more respectable, better-paying career. He liked it just fine at Upward Bound. Carlos told me and Jorge one day that he had saved up enough to buy a kayak. He had a group of friends who were into outdoorsy things, and he enjoyed being out on the water. I entertained myself with fantasies of being one of Carlos's outdoorsy friends. I don't know if Jorge did that, too, but the gentle bear loved to hear Carlos tell stories about his weekend of hiking or kayaking.

I admit that I had unflattering feelings of jealousy when I observed moments of connection between Carlos and Jorge. It wasn't just that they naturally drifted toward each other during activities. Or that Carlos had eyes in the back of his head, looking out in case one of the bullying guys snarked at Jorge. Not all of us here are nonspeaking, and some use their powers of speech for evil. There was one day when a mean jerk was mocking Jorge mercilessly.

The jerk probably gets crap from typical guys all the time, but here he's an alpha dog and takes out his frustration on a guy who can't. Carlos came out of nowhere and moved in on the bully. He's not allowed to manhandle the clients, but he has this Zen way of getting in between oppressor and oppressed and de-escalating a tense situation. He drew the bully away and quietly corrected him, allowing him to save face, while Jorge slumped off. That wasn't what made me feel envious. It was a half hour later. I saw Jorge sitting with his head down, and Carlos was sitting next to him, not saying anything, not even looking directly at him. He was just there. It was a static tableau that communicated the entire scope of their relationship. Jorge takes comfort in Carlos, and Carlos comprehends what Jorge needs without language.

Imagine how ridiculous it was for me to be envious of Jorge, who couldn't even type, much less sit and learn in a proper classroom. My AA degree looked small and useless in the light that emanated from this contented pair of souls. It made me think of me and my mother. We could also be found at the end of a long day, sitting in silence with our heads hung low. Only there was no peaceful contentment, at least not yet. Maybe never. It wasn't that Mom hated her new job, although she probably did. And it wasn't about the downsizing and economizing we had to do now. It was the absence of the happy disruptions that my dad brought to our days, which were now flat and way too consistent. Autistic persons love routine, but I always appreciated how Dad busted me out of my OCD patterns with his nudgy protestations of love. I'm not sure what my mom's version of this feeling was, but she looked as if she had been bullied by life itself, and I wasn't up to the caretaking role that Carlos played with Jorge.

I was feeling sorry for myself. I had good reasons, no question. Here was this big galumphy guy, whom I had every right to feel superior to, and I envied him. The bottom of the barrel wasn't low enough for me. I was going to have to invent a whole new metaphor to describe how worthless my life had become. When I was in high school, and especially at community college, I had a mission. I was a speech-free guy with autism up the wazoo, but I could type and prove that I was as smart as anyone. I was special, in a good way. Now, more than I had felt in years, I was special ed. I had no way of letting people know who I was, and my exterior presentation led people to make demeaning assumptions about me. My intelligence was like the rock pushed up the hill by Sisyphus. I could never get it to the top.

*

It seemed like forever, but finally and abruptly, the main back door blew open and Carlos and Andy rushed out. Now there was a little urgency. Andy ran toward the entrance to the street. Carlos slowly walked over to me. Like in case I was scared or skittish, he didn't want to startle me. I was fine, I was just glad it was Carlos. I tried to point to where Jorge was, but my body wouldn't cooperate. I also tried to summon a non-echolalic word, like "tunnel" or "Jorge," but my mouth wouldn't work, either. Finally I just got up and walked over to where Jorge lay. Carlos said very gently, "Hey, buddy, been looking all over for you." Jorge was happy to see Carlos. He got up out of the tunnel with a smile on his face.

"C'mon, guys. It's snack time."

The three of us walked back to the rec room, where the tension level was a lot higher than when we left. Dave was there, trying to question the clients about where we were, but that didn't seem to be going well. A staffer saw us and cried out. "There they are!" People rushed toward us, but Dave stepped in and had Carlos take us to Dave's office. Dave sat at his desk with a serious look on his face.

"I hope you realize what a dangerous, thoughtless thing you did today. At Upward Bound our priority is the safety of our clients. I can't do my job if you leave without permission."

Dave was like a school principal chewing out a couple of truants. I stopped listening. The people who deserved a lecture were the staffers who weren't doing their jobs. I'm sure they covered their asses, while I was helpless to explain what had happened or to defend myself.

"I am going to have to file an incident report on both of you. I'll send a copy of it home."

An incident report from an adult day care center doesn't sound like a big deal, but it is. An incident report leads to more restrictions, and too many of them means that they send you to a different place. There are worse places than this. If this facility is a run-down bore, the place for adults deemed too aggressive for run-down boredom is closer to autism jail. Wouldn't that be ironic, to go from college to lockdown because I helped them find Jorge. Carlos, bless him, seemed to have a clearer view of the event.

"Dave, I don't think these guys were intentionally breaking the rules. I think Jorge needed a time-out, and Walter was looking out for him. Walter showed me where Jorge was."

That took away a little of Dave's bluster. "Well, Jorge should have let someone know he needed a time-out." That ridiculous statement hovered in the air like a stinky fart. The more you thought about it, the worse it got. If Jorge could let anyone know anything about him, he probably wouldn't need to be here. Ahem, me too. But I'm coming off okay in Carlos's telling, so maybe I'll be spared.

"Well, I guess that's possible," Dave said. "But still, we have to be consistent. They broke the rules big-time, and I'm obligated to file incident reports. I could be the one in trouble if headquarters found out." Dave filled out the reports while Carlos returned Jorge and me to the general population. At least the staffers were being more attentive. They knew this had been their fault, even if they hadn't been held accountable. It was a long day.

When Mom came at 5:45 to pick me up, Dave was waiting for her in the lobby. He took her back to his office. She came out a little later with the report and a stressed face. She barely looked at me until we got home. It took restraint for her to not start yelling at me, I could tell. I think she knew not to take Dave's version of events at face value. She got the letter board and had me sit in our spelling space, a small desk in a small study set aside for the purpose.

"Okay, tell me what happened today. I don't know what to think until I've heard your side of the story."

It took me a while to spell it out, but I was so grateful that I could.

"STAFFWASGOOFINGAROUNDJORGE LEFTTHEBUILDINGANDIFOLLOWED TOMAKESUREHEWASOKAYISHOWED CARLOSWHEREHEWAS."

Mom looked relieved.

"I knew it had to be something like that. I am so proud of you. You deserve a medal, not a report. I'll call Dave tomorrow and explain it to him. Is that okay with you?"

"NOPLEASEDONTDAVEDOESNTGET MEHEWONTBELIEVEYOUJUSTLEAVE ITBE."

"Wow, okay. I guess I get it. What this tells me, though, is that we have to come up with a better situation for you. I wish I could snap my fingers and a magical, perfect place would appear."

She held up the board for me to respond.

"MOMYOUKEEPLOOKINGIAMSKEP

TICALFORNOWTHEMAGICALPLACEIS RIGHTHERE."

I knew that would make her feel better. Her burden and mine are yoked together. We sat in our study space and leaned our bodies and heads gently together.

TOM THE MOVIE STAR

The burly care provider (Victor this morning) lifts Tom out of bed and places him with surprising gentleness into his chair. Tom takes his first pee of the day in the toilet. He tries to poop then, too, because he'll be in a diaper for the rest of the day and he'd rather not make someone else have to deal with that. Tom has some use of his arms, but not enough. Until he was twelve, his mom was able to lift him out of his chair. He didn't weigh much as a kid. He's an adult now, and taller. He has a small army of caregivers who help with one thing or another. They come and go in shifts. They also come and go. Tom thinks he'd have less turnover if he could chat and form bonds with them. The same cerebral palsy that makes his muscles and joints stiff as concrete also freezes his face and mouth. He can't speak a word and can't express emotions. He has them, god knows he has them, but he holds even the most benign feelings inside like a well-guarded secret.

Tom's day begins. Victor wheels him out to the kitchen,

where his mom has cold toast waiting. Victor helps him get it to his mouth. Some days he feels loose enough to get a piece to his mouth himself, but today is not one of those days. Tom's mom and dad are divorced. His dad used to help schlep him around, but after Tom turned eighteen, his visits decreased. His mom works full-time, and he knows she's looking for some kind of residential setting for him. She's done with the day-to-day chore of him. He doesn't blame her. Part of him even looks forward to some autonomy. But it's also scary. People don't realize that he can hear and understand everything said around him, so he has heard a lot of negative comments about how people like him are treated out there. He can't fight back. He literally can't stand up for himself. He can't speak to any abuse. He can only hope that no one takes advantage of his vulnerability in order to work off their own pain.

Victor waits outside with Tom until the little yellow bus from Upward Bound arrives. The act of getting him on board takes a long time. The driver puts out the little red hand on the side of the bus that tells passing drivers they are supposed to stop for the disabled person boarding. Very few cars actually stop, but Tom thinks they slow down a little. The driver comes around—it's almost always a nice lady named Betty—to open the door at the rear and lower the lift. The lift is excruciatingly slow both ways. Tom doesn't mind for himself. He's got nothing but time. He feels bad that able-bodied people have to sacrifice some of their precious hours on the planet to help him live his less-than-precious life. These are his thoughts as he, Victor, and Betty stare at the lift as it creeps along. Once he's on the bus and Victor wheels him into his spot, Betty locks down his chair and gets back in the driver's seat. Tom is always picked up first, for reasons that are not entirely clear to him. He sits patiently as the other five clients in his area are gathered. How else is he going to sit, but patiently? It takes an hour and fifteen minutes to reach Upward Bound this way, whereas it takes his mom about ten minutes to drive there. Tom doesn't mind. At least he's out and can look out the window.

There's no sense in describing what Tom does all day in any detail. They wheel him around from one activity to another. He can't really participate in any of them. He just watches. Sometimes the staffers forget to move him and he just sits by himself until someone spots him. It's a little demoralizing, but Tom decided long ago that feeling bad about his predicament only makes him more miserable. Tom is particularly sensitive to any changes in routine or personnel, either at home or at Upward Bound. He mostly looks forward to these modifications, as the novelty gives him something to think about. His inert body also responds to change. He twitches a little, and his mouth makes a sideways gaping grimace that looks like a drunk person yawning. The problem is that his caregivers, including his mother, interpret his involuntary movements as a negative response to change. So they attempt to minimize any alterations in his routines and caregivers. As if the monotony was comforting. If he were ever blessed with some means of communication, the first thing Tom would tell them is, "Please, for god's sake, mix it up! Take me somewhere I've never been! Show me a movie I've never seen! Introduce me to strangers!" But until that glorious day, he has to appreciate any little spot of newness where it arises.

Today turns out to be one of the most precious days of novelty that Tom has experienced, and no one can shield him from it. It's summer, and there's always some staff turnover in summer. College student part-timers go home for the summer break, while kids who attend college elsewhere come home and need summer jobs. So it's common to come in and see a new face. Today a girl named Ann has appeared. Dave seems excited to have her. He introduces her to the other staffers as the new lifeguard. Time in the pool is a big part of the day during the summer, so this is good news. Tom wonders why Dave doesn't introduce the new girl to the clients, too, but he's not surprised. Things are rarely conveyed or explained to the clients, as if they don't really need to know what is happening in their universe. Tom is watching Dave hand off Ann to Carlos for a tour and some training. She looks overwhelmed but is trying to appear confident. Tom can always tell when a staffer is a newbie to the disability game. They are afraid to look at us straight on. *They are not so much scared of us,* Tom thinks, *but they feel inadequate as to knowing what to do.* This usually annoys Tom, but he feels optimistic that Ann will work out.

Tom waits patiently through the morning activities. Swim time comes after lunch. The sun doesn't hit the pool until noon, and Dave doesn't use the pool heater, so even in summer it's chilly in the morning. Tom's twisted body prefers warm water, but even at a lower temperature he finds relief from the rigidity of his muscles. He has to wait for Carlos to come get him and change him into his bathing suit. Everyone is already in the pool when Carlos wheels him out. Andy helps Carlos with the lift that lowers Tom into the water. It is as excruciatingly slow as the bus lift. Tom sees Ann up on the lifeguard chair looking cute and athletic in her Speedo one-piece. She is staring intently at the lift operation. At least Tom knows she has noticed him. He would be flattered, but that would be ridiculous, and she is clearly trying to make sense of the machinery that gets a wheelchair person into the pool. Carlos goes into the water with Tom and holds him up by his armpits. Carlos uses as light a touch as possible to give Tom the feeling of freedom in the water. Tom forgets the new girl as he floats in weightless calm. He is aware that there are others in the pool, but Tom has an advanced ability to shut out the noisy, bumptious world. He can hear Drew showing off for Ann with all his words, but he is especially good at tuning out Drew's verbal repetition. Swim time is over too soon. Tom endures the chore of getting back into the chair and dressed again. He hopes Ann feels good about her first day.

    Tom thinks about Ann at home that night. Tom sits in his chair while his mom watches TV. He has tried to convey to her that he really likes sitcoms from the seventies and eighties, like *The Golden Girls* and *The Mary Tyler Moore Show*. He thinks she's selective about what she understands, because she exclusively watches true crime shows. He always knows who did it five minutes into the program. Good thing he can't spoil it for her. He fantasizes about what it would be like to have Ann for a girlfriend. He doesn't usually allow himself to indulge in such imponderables. It's painful to dwell on something he can never have. In this situation, strangely, he can't help it. He imagines that he saw Ann looking at him, not just while he was being laboriously lifted in and out of the pool, but afterward, too. He imagines that she looks at him the way a girl looks at a boy she thinks is cute. He's been told that he has a nice face, but he always hears ". . . for a guy in a wheelchair" after it. He feels as if the chair is less primary to Ann. He knows he's being delusional, but what if it's just a fraction of a bit true?

Alfredo arrives. It's his shift to bathe Tom and get him ready for bed. The routine takes about two hours. When Tom was small, his mom and dad performed the job as a tag team. Back then, his mom used to read to him in bed. She stopped a long time ago. Tom thinks she started to believe what his teachers said about him being retarded, and she figured there was no point. Tom thinks she should have known better. Maybe she just got tired of everything. Tom knows something about that. After Alfredo gets him situated for the night, he smiles and says, "Sweet dreams, man." Tom smiles/grimaces back, or imagines that he does. That night, he actually has sweet dreams. Either Alfredo has supernatural powers, or Tom finally has somewhere beautiful to go.

Tom is in a pub in England, or so it seems. He's dressed in country clothes and is wearing a tweedy newsboy cap. He is chatting with some older farmer guys when the old oak door flies open, letting in a gust of wet, cold wind. Into the pub burst three young women, laughing and huddling together. It's hard to see them at first with their jackets and scarves. They peel off their outer layers as the crusty men in the pub steal glances. One girl heads to the bar to get their drinks. She squeezes in between Tom and the sheep farmer next to him. She leans way over the bar and says, "Three pints of Guinness, please." Tom can smell the rain in her hair. She is just turning to give him a big smile when—

"Good morning, sleepyhead," Victor says, and nudges him. "You look happy to see me."

Tom manages to make a kind of gargle sound in lieu of a laugh.

Later that morning, Tom gets wheeled to Ann's table on the patio for a game of Connect 4. He usually checks out during an activity like this. He has a little repertoire of fantasies that help him get through the day. He gets his scenarios from bits of shows and stories he's been exposed to. Sometimes he's the handsome young doctor at the big city hospital. Sometimes a firefighter, sometimes a baseball player. Girls—nurses or groupies—swoon over him, but always from a distance. He recalls his dream from last night and wonders where his subconscious came up with that one. That was the closest encounter he's had with a female in his fantasy stories. Today, at Ann's table, he can't summon any of his usual escapes. Ann keeps talking to him. Talking at him, more accurately. He knows she's new and doesn't know any better, but he's not accustomed to people addressing him so much. It's obviously awkward to keep talking at someone who never answers and who doesn't appear to hear or understand you.

"Hey, Tom, which row should I put this bad boy in? Drew is kicking my butt here."

"Tom, if you move three inches to the left, you'd block the sun from my eyes."

Tom wonders why she doesn't move his chair herself if sun blocking is her objective, then he realizes that she's kidding. She's teasing him. Nobody ever teases him. It's like there's this invisible line of disability, where if you're on the wrong side of it, not even the bullies will make fun of you. You're so far gone that there's nothing funny about it. Having Ann tease him is a weird, new sensation. At first he doesn't like it. But she keeps doing it. The hour session on the patio flies by. He realizes that he was engaged at the table the whole time. Ann may have no experience with people like him, but maybe that also means that she doesn't know the rules and doesn't know when she's breaking them. He decides to keep an open mind about it.

Tom's chair is parked on the periphery of the parking lot while clients are playing basketball. He's not really watching. He's mostly trying to control his head and neck muscles so that he can get some sun on his face. Suddenly Ann appears from behind him, bouncing like the basketball. She's brimming with energy as she crouches on the asphalt and looks up at him. Another new feeling. Tom realizes that people are almost always looking down at him. Even when seated, Tom is physically shorter, and typical people sit straighter and taller. Ann's sacrifice of kneeling is comforting and a little thrilling, even though Tom is certain that the action was unconscious on her part.

"Hey, Tom, are you going to hit a three-pointer from here?"

Tom is ready for her joke this time. He wants her to see that he gets it. All he can manage is his grimace/yawn move with a kind of low-pitched cat sound. Her face lights up.

"Oh, you thought that was funny, huh?"

Oh my god, Tom thinks. *I'm having a conversation.*

After Ann has been at Upward Bound for a few weeks, Tom knows that he's not imagining things. Ann really does seek him out. He doesn't understand why. He has never been anyone's favorite before. He has so many needs and so little to give in return. The weird thing about Ann is how their interactions feel almost reciprocal. She tosses a little comment at him, and then she waits and watches. It's as if she can read the little twitches he is able to make. Most people don't have the interest or patience to focus on him like that. Not even his mother. She stopped really looking at him several years ago. He had a medical evaluation when he was eighteen. In hindsight he realizes that it was intended to determine whether insurance would pay for the physical therapy, speech therapy, and occupational therapy he had been subjected to his whole life. The school district and the Regional Center had been providing it up to then, but at age eighteen everything goes away.

He's right there in the room when the doctor says to his

mother, "I'm sure you're aware that patients with the spastic quadriparesis form of cerebral palsy have shortened lifespans. Tom is not likely to experience any significant improvements in mobility or independence at this point. You may want to start looking for a residential placement where he can be comfortable for the time he has."

The time I have? thought Tom. *How much time have you got, Doctor? Or you, Mom? How much time is the right amount?* Tom is not as concerned about his longevity as he is about quality. He wants his life to be more than a long (or short) slog of painful dependence and helplessness. But there is no cure for what ails him, and the powers that be determined that there is no point in throwing away any more money for therapies to help someone who can't be helped. It was at about this time that his mother stopped looking at him. A part of her detached, as if he were already in some institution or group home. She had already said goodbye, maybe I'll see you on Sunday. Tom is used to living within himself, but he still misses her.

Tom has always been neutral about the weekly field trips to Target. He likes being out, but every Friday is the same, and every routine can become routine. That is, until Ann joins the odyssey. That was one of her jokes.

"Wow, we really put the 'odd' in odyssey," she mutters in Tom's ear as the ungainly group shuffles through the store. She had to prove herself before being allowed to take part. Dave trusts Carlos, and Carlos trusts Ann. She makes the outing more fun, not just for Tom, but for all of them. She insists on pushing Tom, which makes him feel special. He so often considers himself a chore, but she acts as if pushing his chair is a stroke of luck. She pushes while bending over his head. She whispers subversive little comments about people and things they see.

"Who needs a mountain meadow in their washing machine?"

"So should we get the pink champagne or the Manischewitz for tonight, dear?"

"I think the pajama bottoms are a rockin' lewk for a Target Friday. Let's both wear them next week."

Tom scrunches up in rigid-limbed delight when she cracks him up like that. Ann likes to put her feet on the back of the chair and ride along with him. One Friday, Jorge wanders from the group. This is not unusual. Ann volunteers, "Tom and I will fetch him, never fear." Ann takes off, pushing Tom. She leans over him and says, "We both know he's in the toy section, right? Let's take the long way and give him a minute of self-determination."

Ann pushes Tom fast down the aisles that are deserted on a Friday morning. Office supplies, party goods. She gets a full head of steam going, then puts her feet up on the chair. The two of them fly free down the aisle. Tom is in a state of joy. He never gets to do anything naughty, and the speed! Ann makes a wide, fast turn around the store and comes to a screeching halt next to Jorge, who is predictably in the preschool toy aisle.

"Hey, Jorge," she greets. "How are Mr. and Mrs. Potato Head?"

Jorge, being nonspeaking, doesn't respond. But then, he's in a Potato Head–induced trance. Ann gently tugs him away, and the three of them take their time finding the rest of the group.

Tom looks forward to pool time. After she finds her sea legs, Ann makes the pool her monarchy. She jokes around while staying vigilant about safety. Carlos is in the pool with Tom when he is called away. Ann offers to take his place so Tom doesn't have to get out, too. Tom feels Ann's surprisingly strong arms slip around his armpits to hold him up. She floats him all over the pool and somehow creates a kind of conga line flotilla of funky swimmers, Tom at the head. Tom revels in the spontaneous game. His activities are always planned and polite. Ann makes him feel like a whole person, not a chair. He thinks about her when he's at home, and he is always on the lookout for her when he's at Upward Bound. It's the happiest he's ever been, no question. The only thing that darkens his heart is the awareness that she is only there for the summer. She will go back to her college in August.

Tom begins to develop a new fantasy. It starts as a vague idea and gathers details as he goes. His hope is that this story will help sustain him after she is gone.

In this fantasy, for the first time, Tom is in the chair. All his previous scenarios have him strong, tall, and able-bodied. Ann is just like Ann, but she's not in college anymore. She has a cool job and, whatever it is, she works from home. Home is a nice apartment that she shares with Tom. She does some caregiving of him, early in the morning and at night. Together they have organized a program for him that fills his day with positive action. She assists Tom in finding funding for therapists, because the speech, OT, and PT did actually help him. The best part of this shiny new life is that they found this smart college kid who comes in for a couple of hours every day to read to him. This guy takes Tom on walks and talks about trees and insects and other interesting things. The guy (Tom calls him Thomas in his fantasy) is working on a project at school, building a device that would enable Tom to communicate by blinking his eyes. Tom has heard that Stephen Hawking had something like this. Tom and Ann have already been using eye-blinking as a basic means of communication. One blink for yes, two for no.

"Do you love me?" she asks, already knowing the answer. Tom blinks once.

When he opens his eyes again, Tom is looking up at Victor's benign face.

"Hey, handsome, time to rise and shine."

Tom's new fantasy is less idealized than the doctor or firefighter ones, but it's perfect. He feels like more of a hero than before. Then it hits him why this fantasy scene is so important: It's actually feasible. He'll never be a firefighter, he could never become a doctor. And Ann will most likely never be his real-life girlfriend. But he is actually capable of controlling his eyelids. He tests it out when Victor is helping him eat breakfast.

Aides have a way of asking questions of a nonspeaking person, knowing they can't answer. Tom decides to try an experiment. When Victor asks a facetious yes-or-no question, Tom responds by blinking as loudly—as obviously—as he can.

"Still hungry, my man? Want another piece of toast?"

Tom works hard to angle his face toward Victor and he blinks as big as he imagines a clown would do, twice. He realizes that Victor isn't really looking at him. He tries again—blink blink—but Victor has already turned to get the toast. Okay. It's proof that people don't really look at each other, or maybe proof that we are dependent on the spoken word to communicate. Tom decides then and there that he is going to practice his blinking at every opportunity until it becomes automatic. He'll work on consistency and response time. If he keeps doing it, someone will eventually notice. Won't they? A speech therapist could work out a system for him if he ever got taken to a speech therapist again. The thought of this deflates Tom. But he commits to blinking, because what else is he going to do.

Tom blinks his way through the day at Upward Bound. He moves his head, too, as best he can, to call his attention to his face. This, Ann notices.

"Are you showing me your best side, you handsome thing? Are you ready for your close-up?"

Tom blinks twice. She doesn't get it. He blinks again, but she's up and moving now and not looking at him. *This may be harder than I thought,* thinks Tom. He keeps blinking at every yes-no question lobbed futilely at him throughout the day. He notices how often people talk at him this way without even trying to look for a response.

"Are you all done with your snack, Tom?"

"You wanna come sit at my table for craft time, Tom?"

"Did someone leave you all alone in here, Tom?"

Two blinks. Two blinks. One blink.

As much as Tom has spent most of the summer thinking about Ann, his thoughts are now taken over by the thin slant of sun that has appeared. He sees the light of communication in the darkness of his day. He just needs someone to notice. He naturally, naively thought it would be Ann. He even worked it into one of his fantasies. They would be at a table playing Sorry when she would playfully ask him, "Should we move this guy or that guy, Tom?" And he would blink once and she would catch it. "Wait, what? Did you just blink on purpose?" Tom would blink once again, and he'd be off to the races. Ann would show everyone what he could do. She'd demonstrate for Tom's mom and his mom would cry. She'd find a therapist to develop the skill. He'd finally get the chance to study something, get his GED. He'd appear at conferences, maybe write a book. Tom focuses hard on this, his best fantasy, that isn't so fantastical.

The time is getting closer to when Ann goes back to school. She still clearly focuses her attention on Tom, but not in the way he needs her to. He is good at tracking people's emotions thanks to being so still and so quiet himself. Ann genuinely likes him, although he is hard-pressed to understand why. But he senses a slight detachment, not just from him, but from her whole Upward Bound experience. Part of her is already back in her dorm room and her classes and with her friends. And boyfriend? She has never mentioned a boyfriend, but that doesn't mean there isn't one. It's like a slow goodbye. Tom doesn't blame Ann for not picking up on his blinking, but it helps him in detaching himself. He's going to miss her, but he's finally got a job to do, and apparently he's going to have to do it on his own. Blink.

August wends on. It's hot and the pool feels especially good. Ann isn't as much fun as before, so some of the magic has drained out of it. As Tom floats around, held up by Carlos, Ann looks out at the sea of broken bodies, looking for potential disasters. She sees Tom, but she doesn't see the catastrophe in his eyes. He turns away as Carlos flips him on his back. She continues to scan blindly. Dave doesn't plan going-away parties for staffers, much less for summer people like Ann. People say he underplays staff departures so as not to upset the clients with impending loss and change. Dave needn't worry. Upward Bound clients have lost more aides, therapists, and caregivers over their lifetimes than Dave can imagine. Tom certainly has. Losing Ann is different, but not unimaginable.

The day finally arrives. Tom thinks it would be like a Hollywood movie for Ann to have an epiphany about his blinking as she is heading out the door. Too much like a movie. He tries not to let his disappointment spoil his day. It makes him feel special when Ann conspiratorially takes him to a quiet spot to do a selfie. Phones aren't allowed, and neither are unauthorized photos of clients. It's not like Dave is going to fire her today. He feels a little less special when he sees her taking other clients out for secret selfies. And he'll never see his picture with her anyway. It's not like Ann has his mother's phone number to text it. Tom does his best to get through the day. When the time comes for her to leave, she seeks him out. She crouches down and looks up into his face.

"Oh, Tom. I'm so glad I got to meet you."

Blink.

"I'm going to miss you, more than you can imagine."

Blink.

"I hope you will be happy. I'll be thinking of you."

Tom doesn't bother blinking again. He can tell that Ann is emotional, but he has no other means to express himself in return. He feels his stiff body withdraw into itself, making him smaller. And then she is gone.

Everyone is busy then. Staffers see Ann off. Buses arrive. Tom's bus is always last, so he's left in the rec room by himself. Then Carlos comes in, apparently looking for him. Instead of wheeling him to a bus, Carlos takes a folding chair and sets it down in front of Tom. Carlos looks right at him.

"Tough day for you, buddy."

Blink.

"She's a nice girl. She likes you a lot. But that doesn't help right now, does it?"

Blink blink.

"Hey, Tom, is something up with your eyes?"

Blink.

MARIANA'S DILEMMA

Mariana sat at her desk, staring blankly. The phone call she'd just received was from the county jail. They were not going to press charges against her brother. There was processing to be done, but she could pick him up from the jail after she got off work. Her mind, when she had jolted it from numbness, went first to practicalities. She wouldn't be able to pick up her kids from day care. She called Tia Carlotta to cancel their plans. They were going to look at wedding dresses.

"So, sweetie. What are you going to do? At some point Carlos is going to have to pick himself up, solve his own problems. He's a good boy at heart, I know, but you're going to have your own kids to worry about."

"I know, Tia. But he doesn't have anyone else."

"Just don't let him take you down."

Mariana went through her day on autopilot. She sat in her tiny office and did a stack of paperwork she had been avoiding. When her legs went to sleep, she got up to stretch them. She wandered into the rec room to see what the clients were up to. It wasn't her job to deal directly with them. She was strictly an administrative assistant. But she enjoyed watching the clients. Their disabilities didn't frighten her. She'd seen a lot, and she thought she was the perfect person to work here. As she watched the clients, she was occupied with forever worries about Carlos. She knew he was a decent person—she raised him that way—but she hadn't been able to pass along her innate sense of direction. He had none, and she doubted whether he would gain it in the kind of job a young man with his background could get. Fast food, the car wash—if he were lucky. Mariana looked at the young Upward Bound staffers and wondered how they differed from Carlos.

Mariana had been cast in the role of Carlos's mother when she was only eleven. Their mother was a drunk who couldn't take care of herself, much less two little kids. Mariana started out just making sure little Carlos got some food. She took him to school and made him take baths. By the time she was a sophomore and Carlos was in kindergarten, the elementary school used Mariana as the parental contact. Their mother went to prison for robbery when Mariana was sixteen and Carlos was six. The social worker wanted to split them up and put them in foster care, but Mariana showed how well she was caring for Carlos, and they were allowed to live on their own.

Mariana realized with a start that Carlos at twenty was the same age as many of the clients. He seemed older than these autistic men. Boys was what she almost called them. They seemed childlike and so vulnerable. Carlos in a sensitive setting like this would be like the wolf in the chicken coop. She felt that she had failed him at some crucial moment and hadn't known it was happening at the time. She wondered if she could get Dave to hire him. He was strong and could deal with the larger clients. Dave was always looking for strong guys. No. She shut down the thought. Carlos had never held down a job for long. She could only imagine that attitude problems were the least of his flaws. She couldn't risk him hurting the feelings of the clients. And what if he was flaky? That would reflect poorly on her.

Mariana stood in the rec room, no longer seeing the clients. An epic game of ping-pong was taking place in her head. Upward Bound needed male workers. Carlos was male. Carlos was unreliable. Mariana would be here to keep him on track, maybe even on time. Mariana did not have the time or mental space to babysit him. Not that he would tolerate it. What if a client was harmed because Carlos wasn't where he was supposed to be? That's where she got stuck. She would never forgive herself. But what if a job here was just what he needed? What if the clients would benefit from his street smarts?

A shout coming from the clients jolted Mariana from this dialectic. Ben, who has control issues, had had enough of the puzzle activity and swept his arm across the table, bringing a hail of large puzzle pieces into the air. The other clients showed their dismay, and Ben did an evasive dance-like move across the room. There were two female staff present. One tried to wrangle Ben while the other tended to the agitated clients. Mariana quietly stepped into the fray and picked up the jumbled mess of puzzle pieces. She would sort them back into their boxes. She headed back to her office and stopped by Dave's office on the way.

"Hey, Dave. Ben tossed everyone's puzzles again. Should we do an incident report?"

Dave thought for a beat, then said, "If no one got hurt, let's leave it."

Mariana waited and said, "Don't we need some male staff? Ben is too strong for Chloe and Darla to handle."

"I do have to hire someone. Why don't you get me the applications we have on file."

"I had an idea. My brother Carlos needs a job."

"Oh, your brother. I guess any brother of yours has got to be a good guy." Dave smiled his smarmy smile. "Well, why don't you have him come in tomorrow and we'll talk."

"I'll run his background check," Mariana said too quickly. She went back to her office, nervous that this could end badly. She still had to talk Carlos into it. In a deep, silent, unspoiled spot in her heart, Jesus was telling her that it was going to be okay. She grabbed her purse and keys and headed out to retrieve her baby brother.

ANN THE LIFEGUARD

My first day at Upward Bound was like a Kafka nightmare. Instead of waking up as a giant insect, I was a little girl surrounded by alien creatures. I couldn't say this out loud. It's so politically incorrect. Not to mention horribly unkind. Each one of these people is loved by somebody. God loves them. I was nervous and a little scared. Imagine a room full of misshapen young men, not one of whom can walk without lurching. Several were in wheelchairs. Some could speak in words, although to call it conversation would be a massive overstatement. Some were completely silent. Most fell somewhere in between.

I go to college up in Northern California and was home for the summer. My parents insisted that I get a job, although I wouldn't have minded some time off, like you get in elementary school. My dad actually said, "Welcome to adulting. There is no summer vacation in real life." Yeah, Dad, you try keeping up a full load PLUS a job at the bookstore PLUS being on the intermural swim team. I'm a psych major, so I figured I might as well do something I could put on my résumé, rather than Panera or Starbucks. I googled "special-needs summer program." There's not much in my area, but Upward Bound wasn't too far away. I went down there to put in an application. You'd think I was the savior of all mankind the way the director mooned over me. It was creepy but not pervy if you know what I mean. The guy's name was Dave and he reminded me of the nerd with the emu in the insurance commercials. Kind of overearnest, overenthusiastic, super obsessed with the place. He wore cheap office clothes that made me think he doesn't make much money. I understood right away that he needed people badly. That took all the pressure off the interview.

I told Dave that I was interested in working there because I had taken a psych class and learned about autism. That was a small exaggeration. The professor had mentioned autism briefly the day he lectured on abnormal psych. If Dave wanted to hire me on sight, he now saw me as a must-have. I basically said yes before even seeing the place or its clientele. If we had done the tour first, I may have kept walking right out to my car. I was overwhelmed by the sights, not to mention the smells. But then Dave showed me the pool. It was pathetic as pools go, but Dave got all ecstatic telling me how much the clients loved their pool time. I made the mistake of telling Dave about swim team. He nearly passed out in excitement when I mentioned being lifeguard certified. It was decided. I was to be lifeguard when there was pool activity and floater aide when there wasn't.

I wouldn't say the decision was impulsive, but neither was it well thought out. What kind of summer did I have in mind? Not one that involved a bunch of sad, disabled teens and adults. I thought at first that it was all guys, but it turned out there were a few girls, too. I had this impression from wherever that only boys had autism. Why is that? I went home and had a minor meltdown. All I knew was that I had no idea what I was doing. I got lifeguard training for a swim team project, but I barely had enough experience to guard a pool that had a few normal people in it. The pool at Upward Bound had one of those contraptions to lower a wheelchair person into the water. How do you even work one of those things? Would there be someone to show me what to do? How to tell if someone is drowning or just having an autistic spazz attack?

I was stressed out by the time I showed up for my first day. Dave met me in the lobby and introduced me to Carlos, a guy in his mid-twenties who you could imagine had already spent time in jail. The generalizations I made hurt my stomach now. A childhood spent in expensive private schools leads you to make some embarrassing assumptions in the real world. I gathered that Carlos was some kind of supervisor or head aide. Hopefully qualified enough to tell me how to deal with these "clients," as Dave told me to refer to the autistic and disabled people. Carlos surprised me with his competence and chill.

He obviously knew what he was doing, but it was more than that. He made you feel calmer just being in a room with him. I can't tell you how many times over that summer when facing a gnarly situation that I immediately thought WWCD: What Would Carlos Do?

Carlos took me around the place. He rattled off protocols for things like taking clients to the bathroom and cleaning up after them if you didn't make it in time. It was clear that I was to clean up male clients as well as the few females. There was the worn-out little kitchen, the laundry area, the patio and pool, and the locked cupboards with the craft supplies and toys. They used the mostly empty parking lot for basketball, and there was a scruffy little play area in the far back. The clients were all too big and old for that kind of play area. As Carlos explained how the schedule worked, I realized that they basically shuttled the clients in small groups from one activity to another, cycling them through the center's offerings, as pathetic as they were. It seemed sad and boring—the clients looked sad and bored at any rate. It took me a while to figure out that a lack of expressiveness was common and not a true indication of their satisfaction level. Many facts about the clients were only revealed when my vision cleared. It took a little time.

But I was talking about that first day. It still freaks me out how freaked out I was. I might prefer to forget it. But it occurred to me that I ought to have kept a journal this summer. I could use it as part of an honors thesis or something. So in that sweet spot between the end of summer and the start of classes (senior year!) I'm going to try to get down what I can recall of this weird summer.

Before I could even form a cogent question, and I had about a million, Carlos mumbled something and wished me luck. He was gone. I felt like an uninfected person surrounded by zombies in a *Walking Dead* episode. I wanted to run, but I noticed two other staffers going about the breakfast prep. I could identify them by their bright purple T-shirts like the one I was wearing. These Upward Bound tees were our uniform. On the back were several lines that were intended to be aspirational. Looking Past Disabilities, Looking for Possibilities, etc. I'm not sure I saw the possibilities here. I clung to the two other purple T-shirts like a lifeline. I assisted them by lining up the little bowls of cereal for the clients to take. After everyone had some, the two staffers, Chloe and Andy, sat at different tables, so I sat at a third. It was relatively quiet while the clients ate. I was thinking that this might not be as bad as I'd worried.

The first session after breakfast obliterated my brief optimism. It was a gathering of everyone to go over the day's schedule, sing a kindergartenish calendar song, and recite a few facts, like our city, state, country, and who the president is, and the Pledge of Allegiance. The voices of Chloe and Andy were all I could hear. Most of the clients weren't capable of reciting the Pledge or singing the stupid calendar song. The ones that could probably manage it barely mumbled along, as if in a rebellious conspiracy not to participate in the baby routine. I don't know anything about anything, but most of these people didn't strike me as retarded. They were out of control, their bodies didn't seem to follow orders, but there was a flicker of something that suggested that these guys might appreciate a morning routine that was more age-appropriate. I guessed Dave and whoever else was in charge there knew what they're doing.

I was still in a low-grade state of panic when I had to take charge of a small group assigned to play a game of Cootie on the patio. Do you remember Cootie? You've got all these bug parts and you have to roll a die and get a certain number to put the bug together in the right order. I had four clients at my table. I didn't know their names or anything about them. One was a girl. They were obviously familiar with the game, although their grasp of the rules was fluid. One guy snatched up a bug body and started sticking legs in it before it was his turn. Another guy who suffered from verbal diarrhea kept rattling off the rules just as they appeared in the instructions. He knew every word by heart. The third guy just wanted to be told what to do, but his head looked like it was going to collapse from ping-ponging between the rules guy and the no-rules guy. The girl just sat there, quiet and complacent. She didn't make a move toward the game pieces. I tried asking their names. Verbal diarrhea guy switched his word track to naming. The clients at our table were identified rapid-fire. No-rules guy was Ben. He would keep getting out of his chair to jump up and down. I spent half the time asking Ben to sit back down before I just gave up. Head imploder was Isaac, who was black and had dried drool on his T-shirt. Quiet girl was Emma, and I got the impression that the guys were in awe of her. The guy with all the words and names was Drew. He also rattled off everyone's birthdays.

Drew suddenly spit out at me: "What's your name? When's your birthday?"

"I'm Ann," I said, "and my birthday is May eleventh."

"May eleventh," repeated Drew.

He never forgot anyone's birthday, as I came to realize. Cootie was forgotten, however. With a few minutes left of the session, I suggested that we all make the weirdest bug we could. This is probably what made me think of Kafka. Ben sat down for this, but Isaac seemed overwhelmed by too many options. Emma put together something almost pretty. Drew chattered nonstop until I wanted to scream, but there was already enough screaming going on. I got through the morning somehow. My stomach was too nervous for me to eat lunch.

The first session with me lifeguarding the pool came that afternoon. I had no idea what to expect. For one thing, it hadn't occurred to me that the act of getting twenty disabled adults into their bathing suits, along with their towels, goggles, and sunscreen, was a time-consuming logistical challenge. It took virtually the entire staff to facilitate it. There were plenty of people around. I didn't have to worry about being the only pair of eyes on the group. Carlos appeared—thank god—pushing a surprisingly handsome guy in a wheelchair. Carlos called out to Andy to help him load the cerebral palsy guy with movie star looks into the wheelchair-lowering contraption. I was so relieved to see Carlos get in the pool with Tom, the lovely fellow. I'm not likely to forget that name. Several other staffers got in the pool, too. So I'm not responsible for the bodies in motion. I'm just here in case of an actual emergency. That's even worse, in a way. I never thought of myself as someone I'd call in an emergency. Would I even know what constitutes an emergency in a group like this? Once the small pool began to fill up with the funky bodies of the clients and the more conventional bodies of the staffers, I relaxed a little. I started to look more closely at people. Everyone—both staff and clients—had been a blur so far as I had been fighting fear and nerves. Now, as I watched the clients move slowly and awkwardly in the water, they didn't seem as threatening or scary. I have to admit that I had some idea that super-autistic people were aggressive, that they would try to bite me or lash out and hit me.

I still wasn't quite sure of my function at the pool. I saw Emma hovering—hiding—in the corner of the pool nearest my high lifeguard chair. Her eyes were unfocused, swiped to the side. I had the feeling that she was watching me even though she made no eye contact. I called out something stupid, like, "Having a nice swim, Emma?" She receded farther into the corner. I was pleased with myself for having remembered her name.

Drew, still super talkative and eager to please, called out, "She can't talk."

I said, "That's okay. I bet she hears me, though."

I cringed at how lame I was around these poor, odd creatures. How do I talk to someone who can't talk back? Is this girl so retarded that she can't understand what I'm saying? I realized that the clients were not a homogeneous mass of dysfunction. They varied a lot in how capable they were and in what ways they were capable. Stealthy Emma in the corner—who was still staring/not staring/staring at me—maybe couldn't speak, but she was quiet and gentle. It seemed like she was paying close attention to everything, even though she didn't show it. Hyper-verbal Drew, who memorized dates and had fewer physical issues than most of the other clients, looked like he had trouble with impulse control. I wondered if I would get closer to understanding these poor people over the summer. It's a lot different to sit in a lifeguard chair feeling responsible for all these autistics than to read about the disorder in an Abnormal Psych textbook.

The session in the pool was over in a heartbeat. It took them so long to get ready, and even longer to dry off and get dressed again, that the actual time in the pool was short. I felt like I should be helping the other staffers with the task, but I slipped away to get back into my own purple T-shirt and khakis. The thought of dealing with the wet swimsuits and naked bodies gave me the willies. No one seemed to notice that I'd skipped out on the getting-dressed routine. Maybe it wasn't part of the lifeguard's job. Admittedly, this place didn't seem like it was a stickler for job descriptions. Watching Carlos in action was a revelation. He was so quiet and humble, but also confident and competent. He handled things calmly. When a client fell on the bathroom floor while being changed and cut his forehead, Carlos just went into a protocol and everyone relaxed and did their parts. Watching him, even on my first day, taught me something about what leadership is. At college, student leaders were usually the loudest voices. If I were in a real crisis, I would look around for Carlos, or someone like him.

The rest of the afternoon went by pretty fast. I didn't feel comfortable about my performance that day, but at least my anxiety had decreased a little. Over the next couple of weeks, the issue of anxiety came to my attention. I know why I was anxious at first. Upward Bound was a strange, new place to me, and it was filled with strange, new people. But why were the clients so anxious? All they had to do was follow the simple daily routine of playing games and whatnot. I envied their lack of responsibilities. In college I sometimes felt like I had the world on my shoulders. Yet stress and tension buzzed through the place like a permanent live wire. I tried to figure out why. I developed a couple of theories.

1. Autism comes with a side dish of anxiety. It's part of the disorder. Nothing to be done without drug-

ging the person to oblivion. Which some clients were.
2. The atmosphere at Upward Bound was inherently stressful. Too many people in too little space. Autism exponentially magnified.
3. They don't like it here. They would prefer to be doing something productive and age-appropriate. Cootie and crafts as a daily diet are boring.
4. All of the above.

I fell into the rhythm of the place. It was sluggish and hyper, loud and verbally unfocused. The time passed in a blur and days lasted forever. I learned a lot of names, both client and staff, but I wasn't confident enough in my memory to use them. Plus I would be gone in August, so why bother. There wasn't much of a break in the day to hang out with the other staffers. I worked mostly with Chloe and Andy, and we chatted sometimes when the clients were engaged in something that didn't require our hands-on supervision. Both of them went to the local community college. Chloe was studying to become a nurse. She was a first gen-er, the first in her family to go to college. She was driven, like she had something to prove. Andy seemed to be on the eight-year plan. His intention to transfer to university was more stated than felt. I had doubts that he would make it. Still, here we all were, and how judgy can you be about someone willing to do this work?

I was intrigued by Tom, the adorable guy in the wheelchair.

At first glance, he looked like an actor or a pop star. I approached him thinking he would be bright and conversational, just stuck in a wheelchair.

"Hey, Tom. How are you doing today?"

Crickets. He looked at me. It was one of the saddest faces I had ever seen. His natural handsomeness couldn't mask a baseline of frustration. He made a tiny murmur. I saw that on top of his dysfunctional body, he was not able to speak. He wasn't as withdrawn as Emma, but he seemed reconciled to people not talking to him. One-way conversations are difficult to sustain. I made a few more comments to him—at him, really—before I had to go do something. My heart ached for him. Every time I saw him after that, I made a point of getting on his eye level and saying something to him.

"That shirt looks nice on you."

"Are the others too loud for you today? Shall I wheel you over here, where it's a little calmer?"

"Hey, Tom, is this seat taken? Can I sit with you for lunch?"

I am no Florence Nightingale for sure, but a little bit of humanity went a long way with this guy. He had little facial expression, but I could swear that he brightened when he saw me. That's more than I can say about other cute guys I meet.

I also made an effort with Emma. Her mom told me that she liked listening to music, so I would ask questions about what bands she listened to. She couldn't answer in words, but I figured out that if I sang a little of something, she would respond in a way I could understand. Fingers in the ears was a surefire "No." Humming along or smiling was an invitation to keep going. I found her happy place when I sang a little "Yellow Submarine." She obviously loved the Beatles and knew all the songs. Her humming, as tuneless as it was, was right on point. I started listening to more Beatles in my off-hours so I could come prepared. It was fun watching her react.

One activity that I did not look forward to was the weekly trip to Target. It was a community outing intended to desensitize the adult clients to the hustle and bustle of the real world. I had my doubts. Mostly these junkets exposed our people to stares or averted eyes. No one ever bought anything. No one was allowed to, including staff. I couldn't even say to myself, "It's Target day—ugh—but at least I can pick up some deodorant." We just wandered through the aisles aimlessly in a clumpy line. You knew what we were at first glance. I wasn't embarrassed to be seen with the group. I was invisible in my purple T-shirt. I know this because one Friday I spied two old girlfriends from high school in the hair care aisle as our group passed by. They may have recognized me and chosen not to have a big reunion scene right then. It's more likely that our ragtag cluster was below their notice.

I wouldn't have had time to chat at any rate. Half the clients were docile (drugged?) and required only herding. Tom, my glamour guy, wasn't going anywhere without being pushed. I always tried to be his pusher because I liked to lean over his shoulder and make rude comments about people and products. I imagined that we had similar senses of humor. The other half had various behaviors that had to be monitored. One guy would make loud noises, shrieking barely intelligible words and phrases from the videos that seemed to rule his life. You really had to watch him in the DVD section, where the triggers were so numerous that his voice took on even more panic and volume, alarming real shoppers. There were others who managed to wander away from the trail and disappear. This one big guy escaped the group every week. He didn't leave the store, thank god. But Target has a lot of aisles and I got a workout running around to find him. This guy, whose name is Jorge—I'm pretty sure—was always hovering around Carlos at the center. Carlos drives the van and is in charge of the Target run, so he isn't able to pay Jorge special attention on the weekly outings. After a few Fridays of this, I realized that he was in the toy section, or en route to the toy section, every time. After that, he was much easier to find. I would spot him and keep an eye on him, letting him have a little autonomous time to do what he really wanted to be doing. Everyone deserves that. Still, quipping with Tom notwithstanding, Target Fridays were stressful and exhausting. The only positive thing about the field trips was that they chewed up half the day.

As much as I had been anxious about my lifeguarding responsibilities, I looked forward to pool time. I got to sit in my chair on high and it was my personal territory. Everywhere else at Upward Bound I was one of the lowest-ranking staffers. I was just a seasonal hire, which meant that I got assigned the shittiest chores. Literally. I learned to breathe through my mouth and conquer my gag reflex. But at the pool I could lift my face to the sun and breathe in the fresh air. I had authority at the pool. I had a whistle and I used it. Guy running—scuttling, really—on the pool deck? Tweeeet! Guy splashes Emma in the face? Tweeeet! One of life's greatest pleasures is giving orders and having them followed. After the first few weeks of being super serious about the job poolside, I loosened up. I could even focus better on everyone's safety when I engaged with the clients from the chair. Going at it with Drew was easy because he kept up a constant stream of verbosity. But he was low-hanging fruit. I got satisfaction from getting the less verbal clients to react to me. I teased, I flirted. I made both clients and staffers laugh by making up outrageous "Pool Rules" and levying fines and punishments for breaking them.

"Okay, no blowing farts in the pool! Hey, Tom, you're stinking up the joint! You're going to have to pay up! Carlos, bring that guy over here so I can give him thirty lashes!"

The atmosphere at the pool elevated along with my attitude. Clients and staff played spontaneous games of beach ball water polo with me as tyrannical referee. More staffers showed up for pool time. Dave, the director, who hadn't said much to me since he hired me, stopped me in the hall.

"Nice work at the pool, Ann. Love the sass. Just make sure that it's safety first."

"For sure, Dave," I said. "Safety first is my middle name."

He looked puzzled for a second, then burst into a forced laugh. He soon added an additional session of pool time to the daily schedule to accommodate all the clients who wanted to go swimming. The newbies at the pool were the more sedentary clients, so it felt good to see them moving around. Sometimes I got into the pool with Tom when Carlos was busy. I even learned how to operate the ADA pool lift. I enjoyed holding Tom under his arms and swishing him around in the water. He was weightless in the water. His tight limbs relaxed and stretched out. He would sometimes close his eyes, and I wondered where he went in his mind. Does he dream of who he might have been if cruel fate hadn't marked him out? Or was it just me who had those thoughts?

I went home in the evenings with a sense of satisfaction, also complete exhaustion. My mom would ask, "How was work?" in that same perfunctory voice she would use to ask, "How was school?" when I was growing up. She didn't appear to be interested in long anecdotes, so I didn't offer any. Mostly, I couldn't figure out how to explain what I was experiencing to someone who hadn't been inside Upward Bound.

"Fine," I said.

There was a day when things went wonky at the pool. I had been warned that this might happen. I didn't want to believe it. Poop in the pool. You might expect this in a preschool swim lesson, but no one in my pool was younger than eighteen. I had read the protocol for this in the scanty handout Dave gave me at the beginning. When it actually happened, my instinctual response was by the book.

"EVERYBODY OUT OF THE POOL! RIGHT THIS MINUTE!" I tried to keep my ewwwww response to myself, but I may have failed. I gave my whistle a couple of authoritative tweets. I hopped down from my chair and started assisting the clients in getting out of the pool. There weren't enough staffers present at that moment to herd cats back to the dressing rooms, so I was in five places at once. Thankfully, Carlos came to the rescue, and I was relieved to see that he had Tom in tow. I wasn't shy about helping the guys in sensitive situations— I was immune to it by this time—but suddenly I was weirdly reluctant to be around Tom in his most helpless and vulnerable state. The actions required at this moment were very intimate. The only way for everyone to retain their human dignity was to establish a kind of dissociation. I had developed an extra-verbal/beyond verbal connection with Tom that made detachment impossible. This was puzzling, but I pushed it to the back of my mind. Poop was in the pool.

The job of removing the feces from the water was above my pay grade. Or, more accurately, below my pay grade. There is a whole protocol involving a massive amount of chemicals to rid the pool of bacteria. This was not my job, and the pool was closed for the day. I took the ladies to the girls dressing room and I dove into the fray of finding cubbies and clothes. I helped Emma and a few others disentangle themselves from their wet swimsuits and take a scrubby, hot shower to eliminate whatever was in that pool. I brushed out unruly wet hair and did some ponytails. Emma wanted a French braid. I knew that because I had my hair in a braid a couple of weeks before and she was intrigued with it. She kept putting her hands behind her head, but stupid me didn't get the message. Finally she took my hands and put them on her head. Duh. It had become a thing for us. Then the four other girls in the dressing room wanted French braids, too. In spite of the surroundings, which were more run-down nursing home than girlish boudoir, the vibe was fun sleepover rather than post-pool-poop hose-down. I had come to value the level of trust and intimacy it requires to accept this kind of assistance. They, the disabled, were not the other. I was the other, and they had let me in.

The summer sped up. I looked up and there were July Fourth decorations on the rec room walls. I looked up again and it was August. The July Fourth decorations were still up. I went to Dave and asked if I could take them down, put up something more Augusty. He acknowledged my initiative in his smarmy tone and pointed me toward the closet where they kept big plastic bins of holiday stuff. I enlisted the help of Emma, Drew, and some other clients to take the flags and fireworks off the walls. They were unaccountably excited about this chore. Drew rattled off his astonishment.

"We're not supposed to touch those. We're not supposed to touch those. We're not supposed to touch those. Only staff do decorations. May eleventh."

"Yeah, that's my birthday. I got permission from Dave to deputize you guys, no worries, hon."

I hadn't actually asked Dave—it hadn't occurred to me. Judging from the decrepit condition of the paper decorations, I didn't see how the clients could do a worse job than the purple T-shirts. I cranked up some classics on the rec room speakers. Beatles for Emma, Beach Boys for Tom, Taylor Swift for me. The Beach Boys seemed like an odd choice for Tom. I've never met his family, so I don't know if the love of California surf music came from them. One day I had been goofing around with Andy, joking about being a rare native of L.A., and I broke into a verse of "California Girls." Tom was nearby and he nearly spasmed out of his wheelchair. I asked him if he liked the Beach Boys, and he made his go-to guttural noise that I had come to recognize as "Yes." Everybody knows that Drew is a movie nut—along with birth dates, movie opening dates are a verbal tic for him—so I threw in some John Williams. Carlos joined us, along with his faithful shadow, Jorge. They like hip-hop. We're not supposed to play personal music here, but once I had caught Carlos sharing his earbuds with Jorge, and I could hear the thumping bass from where I stood. The clients really liked music, it seemed to me, and that hot August day in the rec room, I wondered why Dave didn't use it to soothe the savage beasts rather than forbid it.

When the Beatles were playing, Emma went into a dreamy sort of trance. She stood facing the wall and swaying. She rejoined us once "Hey Jude" was over. Tom didn't have much facial expression at his disposal, but a certain light came into his eyes when I played "Wouldn't It Be Nice." I couldn't help myself—I grabbed the arms of Tom's wheelchair and wheeled him around in circles like we were at a high school dance. Tom threw his head back and joy emitted from him like sun breaking through clouds. His slender arms, usually held captive in his lap, scrunched up in a cerebral palsied cramp. Instead of reminding me of his disability, the awkward gesture exposed the depth of emotion that was trapped in his stiff body. The crush I had when I first saw his splendid face came roaring back to me as a real thing. The idea of love, the need for love, the practical reality of love, didn't seem incompatible with a wheelchair and an uncooperative body.

Drew kept up his barrage of words and birth dates, but when the theme from *Star Wars* came on, he ran around the room with his arms open like wings, going *bew bew bew*. It occurred to me that Drew had all the spoken words that were denied Tom and Emma, but he was the least mature of them. His wall of words kept him trapped, not allowing him to get beneath or above the empty, repetitious words. Being able to speak was not Drew's superpower. It was his kryptonite.

We got all the paper flags and patriotic stuff off the walls and packed them up. I surveyed the other bins with Carlos and Emma. Carlos pulled out a palm tree and softly said, "Tiki time." Brilliant. I put on some Bob Marley, which animated even slothy Jorge. We scoured the bins for anything vaguely tropical. Carlos got Jorge out of his chair to hang one of those phony fishing nets across the wall. Jorge started giggling for no apparent reason. It was infectious. So corny, but I put on "Don't Worry, Be Happy." It's got that island rhythm. We were all kind of dancing. I looked around at this funny little party and marveled at how much fun I was having. I thought of the last party I had been to up at school, where I drank too much and fretted about how popular I wasn't. This was better.

When we had masking-taped every palm tree, tropical fish, and toucan to the walls, we stood back and surveyed our work. It could not be said that we transformed the ratty rec room into an island paradise. There aren't enough paper parrots in the world to pull that off. Also, the fact that clients were involved meant that rules of order and proportion were not strictly observed. One wall had coconuts clumped together in isolation, and they were too close to a school of sharks and Nemo fish. Some areas had no decoration at all. The imperfections were what made it perfect. You could tell that the clients had done it, and that was more pleasing to the eye than symmetry. If the walls weren't enough to convince you of the rightness, you could look at the bliss on Emma's face. Look at Jorge, still giggling because Carlos was teasing him about the coconuts. Tom couldn't help with the decorating, but his face and body were scrunched up in a nonverbal expression of enjoyment. Changing the script for who could do a certain task had woken us up. The energy we generated had just started to fade when Dave came in. On the speakers just then, a Lizzo song came on. Dave looked furious, but you could tell that he was trying to maintain his benevolent leader demeanor.

"What's going on here?" he said with a strained voice.

Drew piped up, god bless him.

"It's tiki time! It's tiki time! It's tiki time! It's tiki time!"

Dave prides himself on being the Upward Bound party planner, although he sucks at it. You could tell that Dave resented there being an unauthorized bash. He kept his voice under control as best as he could.

"Ann, could you please turn off the music? The rest of you go out to the patio, there's a craft activity waiting for you. Ann, can I see you in my office?"

Carlos wheeled Tom out of the room without looking at me. Tom kept his head turned in my direction as long as he could. He had an adorable face of concern, like I had gotten into trouble on his account. He wasn't wrong. Emma and Drew followed. They had dumb, defeated looks on their faces. I followed Dave down the hall to his dingy office. I knew he was mad, but I wasn't worried about getting fired. The summer was almost over and Dave, as always, was shorthanded. He spoke to me with his wussy version of authority.

"I'm curious as to how you got your personal music on the loudspeakers, but you can show me later."

I suspected Dave was a Luddite, but could he really be that ignorant about how phones work these days?

"You don't have much familiarity with our clients, so let me fill you in."

He proceeded to tell me how their whacked-out sensory systems made it inadvisable to play music because they get overstimulated.

"They get too excited and could harm themselves or others. They could even lash out at you, and I am responsible for your welfare."

What about *their* welfare? What about their quality of life? Where is fun and joy to be found in their lives? I kept this to myself.

"It's also not okay to give them tasks of a practical nature. The risk of failure is too high."

I had to respond to that.

"I'm sorry, Dave. I know you have all the experience. But it looks to me like the clients are bored out of their minds. They seemed to enjoy doing something productive. I bet there's a lot of things they could do around here that would be satisfying to them and helpful to you."

The smug look he gave me was the very picture of misogynist patriarchy.

"I guess you don't know about a little thing I call insurance and liability. I'll tell you all about it if you come back next summer."

Mansplaining gauntlet thrown. Did he honestly believe that there could be liability issues related to taping decorations to the wall? It occurred to me that Dave's rigid rule system was his disability. Otherwise, I couldn't understand how someone could work here for years and not have a clue about the people in his care.

As the day approached that I had to return to school, I felt an impending loss. Like when I went to camp, and when it was over, knowing that I would never experience those people in that place ever again. It was hard to remember how anxious and stressed I'd felt at the beginning of the summer. The disaster I'd feared might occur at my pool—drowning, autistic riot, Tom's wheelchair falling in—never materialized. I'd made friends here, not just other purple T-shirts, but clients, too. Some clients will soon slide from my memory. Others will become permanent installations. Emma's quiet knowing, Drew's efforts to please, Tom's lonely beauty. I was confused about how I felt about Tom. Was I superimposing my empathy for him onto him unfairly? Did we really have a compatible connection, or was I kidding myself? I had no clue about his level of intelligence, but I had read the most imperceptible signs as sparks of understanding. If I am right, what happens to him? Will there ever be a way for him to tell us—tell me—what is going on with him? It was like quicksand, these imponderables.

I recalled an incident from elementary school. There was a very autistic kid in my fifth-grade class. It was clear to all of us that there wasn't much point in the kid's being there. He wasn't capable of the work we were doing, so he sat in the corner of the room with an aide, doing something simple. He made weird noises when he got frustrated, and he got frustrated easily. The aide would take him out when he got too disruptive. Then we wouldn't see him for the rest of the day. The time he would spend in class got shorter and shorter. Seriously, what was the point? One morning, he walked into the classroom, and the first thing he did was grab a chair and hurl it up toward the ceiling, shrieking all the while. I was sitting at my desk in the path of the chair as it came down along with a chunk of ceiling. A chair leg glanced off my shoulder, hitting me hard enough to make a bruise. The ceiling material made a direct hit on my head. The chunk was light and didn't hurt much, but I was startled and let out a scream. The teacher came rushing over while the room erupted in noise and activity. The boy's aide was told to get him to the office. The teacher knelt to assess me. I really was okay, but I was crying. They took me to the nurse's office and made a big fuss over me. My mom came to pick me up and I got to watch TV all day. The autistic kid didn't come to class after that. No one talked about it, but I think we were all relieved he was gone. I'd like to go back in time knowing what I know now. I probably couldn't have helped that kid, but maybe he wouldn't have been so anxious if someone had been nice to him.

My last day arrived before I was quite ready for it. Another of Dave's misguided rules was that no pictures were to be taken of the clients. He took the issue of privacy seriously, but he took it a couple of steps too far. If clients had a good time on a field trip, or made friends with someone, there was no record of it to keep or cherish. Now I was leaving, and I somehow knew I would never come back. I desperately wanted something to remind me of my favorites. I wanted a picture of Tom's beautiful face. I broke the rules. Over the course of the day, I pulled Tom into an unseen corner and took a selfie of us. For a fellow who can't control his face, he managed to look miserable. But then, so did I. I also got shots of Emma and Drew, a few others. Candidly, they were awful. My beloved clients aren't photogenic under the best of circumstances, and I looked puffy and upset. I will never post these on Instagram, not because they are unflattering, but because they are too real for vapid scrolling. Anyway, to post them would only be one of those self-serving plays for praise—look at what a saint I am. Humble brag annoys me and I am not a saint. I'll keep these photos in a file and open it when I need a booster shot of perspective.

So I've done what I set out to do. I've taken stock of my summer. I leave to go back to school tomorrow. I have a feeling that there are going to be consequences that I can't foresee from this close range. That's okay. One thing I'm thinking about is taking a speech pathology class in the fall. I know of one client at Upward Bound who is supposedly able to communicate by typing. I didn't see him do it, but I'm really interested in the potential. Possible career path. I'm having trouble finishing up my packing. I keep looking at the best picture I got of Tom. He literally looks like an angel. Saying goodbye to him on my last day was anticlimactic, but I knew enough by now to expect that. I knew also that my absence would be felt. I may not have access to his words, but his eyes told me. I'm reminded of that phrase they use in memes: Find someone who looks at you the way Tom looked at me the day we decorated the rec room and danced to "Wouldn't It Be Nice."

TEMPLE GRANDIN

Books can't teach you to be a human being. I have listened very carefully to the books my mother has read to me, but there are surprisingly few clues about how to be a human. I struggle with so many of its requirements. Humans are supposed to look out for each other, like poor Dorothea cares for her dear, sour Mr. Casaubon. Good humans communicate with each other in the way that the Misses Bennet, Elizabeth and Jane, did. Exemplary humans fight for something larger than themselves, like Count Nikolai Rostov and Prince Andrei Bolkonsky. But I can't take care of my own damn self, and I can't communicate in a drawing room or anywhere else, and no one would let me near a battlefield. So what constitutes humanity for someone who desperately wants to give but is only devised to take?

There is no sweeping novel, no *War and Peace*, not even a *Pride and Prejudice*, by or about a seriously autistic person. I am unrepresented in the canon. I have found zero role models in literature. The most famous autistic writer I know of is Temple Grandin, but she writes nonfiction. Her intense interest in life is the humane treatment of cows headed for slaughter, and she writes about how she is able to see things from the cow's perspective. That's fine and useful for the cows, but it doesn't help me much in my mission to be more human.

Still, Temple Grandin is a good representative of the autistic community. She is highly educated and successful at being her autistic self in a neurotypical world. That's my goal, too. I was twelve when the HBO film on Temple Grandin came out. It was not a particularly good time of my life. School and hormones hit me hard. I saw previews of the film on TV and felt a weird sense of hope and pride. There were so few autistic people portrayed in film or TV, and none with PhDs. Things were looking up for my people.

My mom had a group of autism mom friends. Some of their kids were at Upward Bound, but not all. They would have coffee or lunch or ladies' nights out and share their adventures raising difficult children. We were the only ones who had HBO, so the moms organized a grown-ups-only viewing party of the Temple Grandin film at our house. The couples ate and drank a lot of wine. I hovered in the background, listening. They talked hilariously about the things their kids did. The failures, the teacher meetings, the IEP battles. Ha ha ha ha, they laughed. I know they were just letting off steam, but it's hard hearing parents (including my own) making jokes about our struggles. Mom got into it with Ian's mom about how both Ian and I have escaped from them in public places. So scary, ha ha, sip sip. I heard Christopher's mom brag/complain about Christopher's implausible dream to become an air traffic controller. How could he ever keep up in a real airport, ha ha, sip, pour.

Finally everyone gathered in the living room to watch the film. I sat in the corner by the picture window. I was allowed to stay. I think my mom figured I'd enjoy it, or she forgot I was there. The movie began, and my hackles went up immediately. Temple Grandin is a memorable person in real life. Big and awkward and ugly, in the way that Eleanor Roosevelt was ugly, magnificently ugly. Yet here was this lovely, lithe actress playing her. The actress tried hard to mimic Temple Grandin's harsh, horsey, flat voice, but it was so false coming from her loveliness. The worst thing about this terrible, insulting film was when they attempted to visually manifest Temple's meltdowns. The special effects made it seem as if she were on an acid trip, or an attraction on the Universal Studios tour where you can see the wires operate the disaster on repeat.

Autistic meltdowns can't be recreated in two dimensions. They are not a horror film. I wouldn't begin to know how to show a neurotypical person what it's like for your mind and body to implode, but this film wasn't it. The pressure was building up. I was getting more upset and angrier by the minute. Then I blew. The next thing I knew, I'd thrust my scrawny arm through the large window in front of me. The glass shattered, some of it falling into the room around me. The adults, looking like a den of meerkats, turned their heads in unison to gaze at me mildly, no shock or panic. They immediately registered what had happened, and the collective response was a seasoned "Well, sure, my kid would do that/has done that." My mom and dad came over to me, not unkindly. Then they noticed my arm. It had been sliced open and there was a fair amount of blood. Fortunately, Christopher's dad is a doctor. He used our first-aid stuff to stop the bleeding and bandage it up. He discussed with my parents whether I should be taken to the ER for stitches. Every parent in the room was familiar with the experience of taking an autistic kid to the ER. Doing it late on a Saturday night was not advisable. It was agreed that I would survive without stitches.

My dad didn't seem entirely convinced by the consensus opinion. He was a bit of a hypochondriac for himself, and he went to the doctor for symptoms that my mom would have ignored. Finally, the Saturday night consideration and the presence of an actual doctor silenced his dissenting voice. He offered to take me upstairs and brush my teeth while Mom cleaned up the glass. Dad put his arm around me while he helped me hold my toothbrush. He talked about the gnarly scar I'd probably have, how it would ward off bullies. He climbed on the bed as I settled in and made sure my arm was safe before giving me a big good-night hug.

The adults settled back down to finish the movie. The room turned chilly from the evening air coming in through the shattered window. I heard the guests leave an hour later, still laughing. I put a finger of my nonlacerated arm in my ear, but it wasn't enough to silence the sound of their camaraderie. The next day, my mom took me to my regular doctor. He didn't think my sliced-up arm was funny at all. He said that there wasn't much point in doing stitches, but that I would have a scar. Dad was right.

I have an impressive disfigurement on my left arm. It is a reminder, like a string around my finger, that there is something I need to do. The story of my people isn't being told, or it's being told wrong. No neurotypical person can tell this story. No lovely actress, no smart but normal writer can tell you what this is like. My scar is a hieroglyph telling me to tell the story myself. My scar is in three dimensions.

DAVE THE DIRECTOR

Dave gets into his grumbling Honda Civic and pulls out of the Upward Bound parking lot. He makes his breathing as slow and deep as he can so the stress that rises from the rush-hour traffic doesn't agitate him. Conquering frustration has been crucial for his job. There is nothing more frustrating than having to deal with an autistic man twice his size in full meltdown, behaving like a ridiculous but dangerous child. Even more frustrating is having to raise funds for the center. Some of the clients' families are well-off and willing to contribute, but it's never enough. He feels like he walks through life with his hand out, hoping a few dollars will fall in. Just like the filthy, unhomed man standing next to his car at the stoplight. Not enough separates him from the ragged man on the median. Dave has a fancy title, but the salary that comes with it isn't enough to cover the bills.

 He drives through McDonald's on his way home. He keeps meaning to get some healthier food in his fridge, but he's always too exhausted after work to cook. Any vegetables he buys end up shriveled and dried out, so he just stopped buying them. Even stoked by junk food, his forty-six-year-old body isn't too fat, so he figures he still has time to clean up his act. He drives south, the houses giving way to apartment buildings that get gradually shabbier. He enters his parking garage and avoids the post that has left marks on his car that aren't worth fixing.

Dave gets his mail from the rusted cubby with the broken lock and uses the stairs so he doesn't stink up the elevator with his McDonald's. He knows he has to eat fast or the french fries will harden into their original chemical state. He sits on the brown sofa and clicks on the TV while opening the messy little packets of ketchup. Of course he gets ketchup on the remote, because of course he does. He also gets some on his short-sleeve button-down work shirt. It was on its third day anyway. He finishes his Big Mac just as the local news is coming on. He's been on the news a bunch of times. That's something that his old high school classmates can't say. Every year, Upward Bound puts on a big fundraising event, and Dave manages to wrangle an aging TV star to host. The star is just big enough and he is just persistent enough to get at least one of the local stations to cover the event. He doubts that the coverage sells any tickets, but having Upward Bound in front of the public eye is always a good thing.

People are not necessarily drawn to a place like Upward Bound when they go to donate. The clients are mostly young adults with autism. If any of them were cute as kids, which is hard for Dave to imagine, they lost that years ago. Upward Bound is the kind of place that people are glad exists so the autistic adults have somewhere to go. They also don't really want to know about it. Hence his difficulties fundraising. Hence him falling all over himself in gushing gratitude to the eighties TV actress who is willing to show up to his annual Fall Festival and have her picture taken. You can usually see Dave in the picture or in the background of the promo spot, but the actress does the interview.

Dave acts very cool during these brief moments of star proximity. He came to Southern California fifteen years ago with ideas of working in Hollywood. He knew he couldn't make it as an actor, even though he had played Boris in a production of *The Cherry Orchard* at Western Kentucky University. He knew he had talent, but he was self-aware enough to know that he was not in possession of movie star looks. That didn't stop him from going to a couple of open casting calls that he found online when he first moved here. Those all turned out to be efforts to get him to sign up for an acting workshop, and he didn't have the money for that kind of thing. He believed that he had it in him to be a director, but he needed a shot. As the *Hamilton* lyric says, he's not going to throw it away. No shot has presented itself, at least not so far. He harbors a secret dream that one of his Fall Festival donors will be a producer who notices how well he manages the big event and will tap him to direct an episode of his Netflix series. Or Amazon, or AMC. It hasn't happened yet, but you never know. One of his clients had a dad who worked at the studios, but the poor man passed away before the client came to Upward Bound. Dave is always nice to the mom in case she remarries someone in the industry.

Big Mac consumed, *Jeopardy!* on. Sometimes Dave knows the answer and calls it out as the contestant buzzes in. It feels good to be right, but he wishes someone was there to admire him. He had a girlfriend for almost a year, but she broke up with him right before the Fall Festival two years ago. He knew it wasn't a forever thing, but he thought her timing was unkind. She knew how important it was to him, and it definitely threw him off his game that year. They didn't have much in common. She didn't like *Jeopardy!*, for example. Seriously, who doesn't like *Jeopardy!*? She said it made her feel stupid. He probably made a mistake when he took her to Upward Bound for a tour. He hoped that she would be impressed with his being the director and voice of authority of the whole place. Instead, she was awkward and uncomfortable and couldn't wait to leave. He tried to look at the building and the clients with an objective eye but believed that there was real goodness in the place. The clients looked weird and there were admittedly a couple guys who could get aggressive under certain adverse circumstances. There wasn't any real reason to feel fear. Everybody there needed to be there, including him.

Dave thought that Sharon could have had a more charitable attitude about it. She went to church all the time—didn't she listen? Dave's not that big of a Christian, but he figures that Jesus would love what he does for the disabled people under his care. In the same way that his autistic clients need a place to go, so does he. He had always had trouble finding a place to fit in. He was bullied in school for looking so goddamned geeky. How was that his fault? His whole family had the same look— kind of pasty and challenged in the chin department. His family never had the money to dress cool, not that he would have known how to dress cool even if they had. His dad had a bunch of different jobs when Dave was growing up in Paducah. He worked in an office at a car dealership. Dad lacked the charisma to sell the cars. Then he worked at a grocery store but quit when he kept getting passed over for assistant manager. He was a mail carrier when he was diagnosed with colon cancer. Dad knew something was wrong when he couldn't get through his route anymore.

Jeopardy! over, Dave surfs around and finds a *Law and Order* episode. He gets reassurance from the predictable formula of the show. He half watches it, remembering the plot from previous viewings. Sharon hadn't liked *Law and Order*, either. She said it was too New Yorky and she couldn't relate. Dave has always wanted to go to New York. He can't remember what he liked about Sharon except that she was willing to go out with him. While *Law and Order* proceeds in its inevitable procedural path, Dave pushes Sharon from his mind by calling up notes on the upcoming Holiday Spectacular on his laptop. Unlike the Fall Festival, the holiday show is not a fundraiser. It costs more to put on than they make from donations. Dave figured out after his first attempt at a holiday show that you can't charge for tickets. Too many clients come from low-income families who won't come if they have to pay. There's nothing more depressing than doing a show with no audience.

Dave loves putting on these shows. He goes down the list of songs and skits to make up the program. No one realizes how hard it is to produce a show like this. About thirty clients participate, most of them willingly. Of those thirty clients, maybe three can be relied on to learn a few lines and recite them on cue loudly enough to be heard beyond the edge of the stage. Of those three, only one has what you might call stage presence. Over the last couple of years, as a result, the Holiday Spectacular has become The Anthony Show. Anthony is a big ham who demands a lot of attention, which can be annoying under normal circumstances. One day out of the year, it comes in very handy.

Anthony was the mascot for his high school's football team, which he never lets you forget. Not an official mascot with a big-head costume. He was an equipment assistant, and the guys joked around with him. Once, during a game that the team was losing by thirty-five points, they let Anthony run a play. A picture of the charitable moment ran in the local paper, and the team was applauded for their generosity of spirit. Dave is cynical about that. He thinks they were trying to go viral on Instagram. That didn't happen, but Anthony has been reliving his triumphant moment on the gridiron ever since. It reminds Dave of that song about the guy in the bar who can't let go of his glory days. It makes Dave sad that the moment will probably remain the greatest accomplishment of Anthony's life. Being disabled sucks. Dave never had anything like a glory day until he came to Upward Bound. Now he's had several of them.

Dave falls asleep on the couch with his computer on his stomach. The next morning, he puts on a clean shirt in honor of the first day of rehearsals. He always wears a tie to work, although the dress code of a center like Upward Bound is casual in the extreme. You have to be ready for all kinds of messes and contingencies. But Dave likes the authority that a tie gives him. He makes the staff wear easily identifiable matching T-shirts to distinguish them from the clients. His tie distinguishes him from the staffers. He gets into his car, counting off the list of things that need to be fixed. His job makes it hard to get stuff like that done. He drives to work feeling like he just left the office a minute ago.

When he gets to Upward Bound, Edith is in her wheelchair, waiting for him to unlock the door. He has the only set of master keys. Another signifier of his authority. Edith has to take the bus to work and she almost always gets there before he does. Every morning he thinks to himself that he should either give her a key to the front door or get to work twenty minutes earlier. Seeing Edith slumped over in her wheelchair in the morning chill makes him feel guilty. Then he reminds himself how lucky Edith is to have a real job, thanks to him.

"Good morning, Edith," he calls out in the cheeriest voice he can muster. "Sorry to keep you waiting."

"That's all right, Dave," she answers. "Bus schedule's fault, not yours."

Edith steers her power chair behind the receptionist's desk and sets about getting ready for the day. Dave isn't sure why Edith is in the chair. He's no doctor and he's never asked her. He takes privacy laws about disabilities very seriously. He forbids staffers from talking to clients or their families about diagnoses, and he shuts down conversations about them among themselves. Edith has a weak, puny voice that annoys him, and she can prattle on if you ask her an innocent question like "How was your weekend?" So he tries to keep chitchat to a minimum. Despite Edith's physical challenges, she doesn't suck as a receptionist. She's probably in her fifties, although she could also be in her forties. She looks drab and haggard, but she honestly enjoys everyone who walks past her desk. The desk is at chest level, but she is shrunken in her chair and can't see over it. Parents, grandparents, and bus drivers go right up to the desk and look down to exchange a few words with her when they are dropping off or picking up clients. Dave tends to avoid doing this.

Mariana enters soon after Dave has opened up. They are

supposed to arrive at eight, prior to being open for clients at eight-thirty. Mariana is usually five or ten minutes late. Dave doesn't like this but she has little kids and he figures she's juggling a lot. She is very attractive and also very sweet. He doesn't feel that being stern with her would be productive. He follows Mariana into her office and starts peppering her with questions and instructions before she's had a chance to put her coffee down or her purse away. She learned the hard way not to leave personal belongings where the clients could get at them.

"So today is the first day of rehearsals. Is the stage area cleared away? Have you printed up the rehearsal schedule for the parents?"

"Good morning, Dave. How are you doing this morning?"

Mariana seems sweetly determined to observe niceties before responding to Dave's urgent concerns.

"I want to make sure that Anthony has his script for today. Could you print another copy in case he forgets his?"

"Sure, no problem."

"And get me the sign-in sheet by ten so I can make sure the clients I need will be here."

Dave is in his office working on staging when Walter's mom sticks her head in the door.

"Hey, Dave, you got a minute?"

Dave likes Walter's mom; she's mostly pleasant and supportive. But she can overthink things. Walter doesn't speak and can't do much in the way of activities. Dave sometimes wishes his mom would just relax and accept reality. But no . . .

"I would really like Walter to participate in the holiday show. He never got to do that sort of thing when he was growing up. It always made me so mad that the schools didn't even try to include our kids. They were trying to make things look professional and forgot about the spirit of the thing."

Dave shakes his head and makes sympathetic clucking noises. Internally he's rolling his eyes. *Have you met Walter?* he feels like asking her. *What do you think he can do?* It always strikes Dave as weird that he has to have these awkward conversations with parents whose kids are adults. About a third of his clients live in group homes. None of those families bug him about stuff like this. The others still live at home, and there are definitely some helicopter parents among them. Dave says all the right things to Walter's mom but wishes he didn't have to deal with it. He knows Walter well enough to know that he would rather spin around in circles in the corner of the room than be onstage singing "Jingle Bells." Not that Walter could sing "Jingle Bells" if he wanted to.

Walter's mom goes away satisfied. Dave sighs as he sits back down and tries to figure out where he can stick Walter where he'll be the least disruptive. It's not that the show needs to be perfect. But members of the Upward Bound board come to his Holiday Spectacular and he feels like he's judged by the result. Oh well, Walter's not the only one in the cast who presents a directorial challenge. Maybe it would help if he stuck some kind of prop in their hands. Something that makes no noise but would be like a fiddle toy to ground them to their spot in the back. Dave wishes he knew more about autism. He got to be the director of Upward Bound without any background in special ed or psychology. He came up through administrative ranks. Now that he's in charge, it would be embarrassing to admit that he doesn't know much about the dominant disability of his clients. He's gotten pretty good at faking it, thanks to his powers of observation. But he spends most of his time in his office, which is as far from the clients as you can get.

Dave keeps glancing at his watch, anxious to start the rehearsal. When it is finally three o'clock, he enters the rec room raring to go. First thing he sees is Anthony pacing back and forth on the edge of the stage muttering to himself as if he's memorizing a soliloquy from *Hamlet*. Then he looks around and sees only about fifteen clients sitting in folding chairs. There should be twice that. He notes wryly that Walter is among the missing. He sends Carlos out to round up the rest of the cast. Carlos is his most reliable staffer and he has a way with the clients. Dave depends heavily on Carlos, a fact that he tries not to let on. He realizes that he should probably give Carlos a title befitting his function, but he worries that having an assistant director would dilute some of his authority. One by one, eight more clients meander in, reminded by Carlos where they were supposed to be. Dave is prickly, irked by the lack of urgency. Anthony is the only one who's come ready to work. He's actually several levels beyond ready, well into the realm of anxious dervish. Dave decides to begin while Carlos rouses the remaining stragglers, including Walter. Dave addresses his cast.

"Hi, everybody. We have a great Holiday Spectacular planned for you this year."

"Yay!" yells Anthony.

"We will rehearse Mondays, Wednesdays, and Fridays at three until the show on December fifteenth. Make sure that your families and caregivers know the schedule. I emailed them the information—make sure they got it. It's very important that everyone is present for every rehearsal."

"Especially me!" cries Anthony.

Anthony's enthusiasm is not matched by anyone else in the room.

"We're all important, Anthony. Everyone has a role to fill."

Anthony continues pacing across the stage self-importantly, but he stops interjecting.

"We're going to start with the opening scene, which includes the whole cast. It's set right here at Upward Bound, with everyone gathering for a holiday party. Art imitating life, as they say."

Dave and Carlos place the clients around the stage according to Dave's chart. Easier said than done. Some can follow instructions and stay in place, but most are like jumpy cats that prowl and slink and leap. Dave starts to get frustrated, but he sees the Zen-like patience of Carlos and is better able to swallow his irritation. They get the opening tableau more or less set up. Walter is in the very back with a few of the other nonspeakers. Walter can't make intelligible words, but he can produce a lot of noise. The poor guy is agitated and makes high-pitched siren sounds almost nonstop. Carlos tries to calm him but has no luck. Dave finally has Walter sit out the rehearsal with staffer Andy standing watch over him. Not only does Walter chew up precious rehearsal time, but his expulsion from the stage deflates the others. They don't get much done in that first rehearsal, but that's why Dave starts in October.

The rehearsals continue and a handful of skits take shape. Since most involve Anthony and a few others, Dave keeps the meetings small most days, even though he'd prefer everyone to be there. It's too much like herding cats. He only calls the entire cast once more before Halloween. Dave is obligated to make a big splash for the Upward Bound Halloween party. A fair number of clients can't tolerate wearing costumes. No big surprise that Walter is among these. Others are in group homes where no one bothers to help the clients put a costume together. But there are enough clients who love Halloween that Dave puts his Holiday Spectacular aside for a few days so that he can throw a kick-ass party. He has his staffers put up the decorations, and Carlos is sent to Smart & Final for candy. Dave dusts off the rec room audio system and locates the CD burned by some long-gone staffer with Halloween hits like "Monster Mash" and "Thriller." Dave invested some years before in a first-class Dracula costume, and he knows he cuts an impressive figure. The party looks great and goes pretty well. The Walters notwithstanding, some of the clients get into the spirit. Anthony busts out a special version of the Michael Jackson "Thriller" dance that is unintentionally hysterical. The party starts at three and is over at five, when the short buses arrive to take clients to their group homes and the parents come for the others. Dave tells his staffers to come in early tomorrow morning to clean up and take down the decorations so they can restore the rehearsal space to its distraction-free state. Dave goes home, takes off his scary makeup, hangs up his Dracula costume in its protective garment bag, and treats himself to a beer. He has a dream that night about Santa's beard catching on fire.

Now that the Halloween detour is over, Dave commits Upward Bound fully to the Holiday Spectacular. He has non-cast members making little craft items for props and decorations. He recruits staffer Andy, who plays the piano, to run through the songs with the whole cast. Dave chose the easiest Christmas songs to remember and to sing, like "Jingle Bells" and "We Wish You a Merry Christmas," but even these still sound ragged and pathetic after three weeks. Dave calls Andy in for a chat.

"So how do you think it's going?"

"Okay, I guess."

"Are the clients learning the songs?"

"Oh, I'm pretty sure they know the songs."

"It didn't sound that way yesterday."

"Yeah, well, like I told you, I'm no choir director. Makes sense when you figure that they have trouble talking, too."

"Maybe there's a video on YouTube or something that shows you how to teach singing to our population."

Andy doesn't respond right away. Dave thought it was a pretty good idea. Andy has a pained look on his face. A long pause follows.

"I'm doing my best, Dave. They're doing their best, too. This is their best. I think it's fine. It is what it is."

"We want our clients to have high expectations for themselves. We want them to strive for excellence. Your attitude is not going to cut it."

Dave can swear he sees Andy roll his eyes. Damn kid. What does he know about striving for excellence. Dave sits in the back of the rec room that afternoon to assess the damage. He notes with irritation that Walter is pacing up and down, not even trying to sing or pay attention to Andy's directions. Others, like Drew and Down Syndrome Isaac, are really going at it. They seem to want to get Andy's attention or approval. Andy is funny with the clients. *That's fine,* Dave thinks, *but you have to have discipline before you can joke around.* Anthony sits in front, closest to Andy. Suddenly, Anthony stands up.

"I don't need to be here. I'm going to go practice my speeches."

Dave sees that stardom has gone to Anthony's head. He follows Anthony out and stops him in the hall.

"Anthony, you have to set a good example for the others. They look up to you as the lead in the show."

"But Dave, it's so borrrring. I can sing 'Jingle Bells' already."

Dave can hear the piano and a couple of tuneless voices coming from the rec room. There are fifteen clients in that rehearsal, but you'd never know it. His shoulders slump in defeat. He puts his arm around Anthony's shoulder.

"Come on, pal. Let's go work on your monologue."

The show starts to come together in its fashion. The skits featuring the verbal clients are okay. Dave cuts one group scene so he can concentrate on the other two. One opens the show and the other closes it. Dave watched the Charlie Brown Christmas special several times while he was writing the show. The final scene inspired him. He'd like to use a Bible passage in his show, but he knows he can't. This is an eclectic group to say the least, and Upward Bound receives some federal and state funding. Dave writes the final monologue himself, going through old Upward Bound brochures and donation solicitations for inspirational phrases. He pictures it in his mind. Anthony center stage in the Linus role. *Maybe I can get him to hold a beach towel to reinforce the reference,* he thinks. Andy as Schroeder at the piano. Emma is the closest thing to a pretty girl Upward Bound has right now, plus she stays where you put her, so she goes next to the piano in the Lucy position. The rest of the cast is scattered randomly around the stage. His clients' dancing isn't that different from the Peanuts kids' nutty movements. *It's brilliant,* Dave thinks. By the final rehearsal, the reality isn't that far off from his imagination.

Dave can't neglect the audience in his plans. He had gotten a call in September from a committee lady for a fancy charity in town that puts on a debutante ball for the rich girls. They always have the debs do a service project to give back to the community that has given so much to them. The lady, whose name is literally Karen, loved Dave's idea that the debs could play hostesses at the Holiday Spectacular. She excitedly took on the tasks of providing treats and ushers. Dave has a meeting with the girls, Karen, and a few of the moms. There is so much female energy in the conference room that Dave can hardly breathe. He is so fully immersed in the challenged world of Upward Bound that he has forgotten that there's a whole other world out there. A world where the girls are beautiful and wear nice clothes. Where girls are bubbly and articulate and enthusiastic and smell so nice. The moms are a little overbearing, but they are here to help, not to demand something unreasonable. Dave gives a little speech about his Holiday Spectacular and what he needs from them.

"Our clients come from all different kinds of homes and cultures. Most are economically disadvantaged, but not all. Their disabilities are diverse, too. Most have autism and intellectual deficits. We also have clients with cerebral palsy and Down syndrome. You don't have to be afraid of them. We will have plenty of staffers present to step in if someone gets too excited. You'll know the staffers by their purple T-shirts. This is a really big deal for our clients. They look forward to it all year. Having you girls here will make it even more special."

"We have arranged a cookie bake and will have about ten girls to man the dessert tables," says Karen.

"We're going to wear super-funny ugly Christmas sweaters to like, be in the spirit," squeals a blond deb. The other girls cackle along. Dave thinks he'd rather see the girls in pretty party dresses, but he hates to squelch their hilarity.

The dress rehearsal arrives. It's not really a dress rehearsal with costumes, as the clients are wearing street clothes in the show. Dave tells them that it's in keeping with the "Charlie Brown Christmas Show" theme, but there's no money for costumes in the budget. There's not actually a budget, per se. If the debs hadn't stepped up, there'd be no refreshments. Money is a constant irritation for Dave. He has so many ideas for events. He'd love to do a big Hollywood Nite with a red carpet and their TV actress benefactor. The clients would love that. But there's no money to do it the right way. It's as much as he can do to meet salaries and keep the lights on. He's going to place a couple of donation baskets around the room on show night. Maybe some of the debs will have a heart.

The rehearsal goes just okay. The clients are either a little hyper or totally checked out. Both are annoying. Dave wishes he could smush the two behavioral states together and lead a cast that was engaged and competent. He does his best to mask his frustration in front of the clients.

"Okay, everybody. Get in place for the finale."

The staffers move the bodies into position. Emma is placed by the piano and Tom's wheelchair is pushed to the front. Dave knows that the wheelchair tugs at the heartstrings. Anthony waits offstage for his big entrance. Andy starts playing the piano. It's not the Peanuts jazz music, it sounds like that Mariah Carey Christmas song, but that's fine. The clients move around awkwardly when Dave yells at them to dance. *Oh god*, he thinks, *tomorrow night they're just going to stand there unless someone prompts them to move.* Dave despairs until Anthony strides out onstage with gusto. He is on fire today. He delivers Dave's cobbled-together speech like it's the Gettysburg Address. Dave feels a swell of hope. You would never mistake Anthony for a real actor, but he's got a disabled brand of charisma that his high school football team must have responded to. Dave recalls the old theater adage about bad dress rehearsal means great opening night. Today's rehearsal was a mixed bag. The Walters in the cast were a mess as usual, but Anthony was a star. Tomorrow could go either way.

Dave drives home feeling better than usual. He picks up a WaBa bowl with brown rice and vegetables instead of his usual burger and fries. After *Jeopardy!* is over, he finds *Love Actually* on a movie channel. The romantic stuff makes him think of Sharon, but not in a bad way. He thinks about calling her and inviting her to the show tomorrow. He's got her number up on his phone but hesitates. It's so last minute. She didn't dig the scene before. He couldn't bear to see the look of distaste in her eyes on what could be a good night for him. He puts down the phone. He watches Liam Neeson and his little boy embracing at the airport. It's heartbreaking and uplifting at the same time. Maybe his show can be that, too.

In the morning, Dave dresses carefully in his sharpest button-down shirt and khakis. He chooses his classiest tie. He keeps his sport coat on its hanger so it doesn't wrinkle. He doesn't make coffee. He's sure he would spill if he did. He greets Edith at the door and doesn't have to fake his cheery greeting.

"I'm sorry I won't be able to stay tonight for the show," says Edith. "If I'm not checked in at the group home by six they give out a penalty."

"I know, Edith," says Dave. Edith's restrictions are consistent. "We will miss you. It's going to be a great show."

Dave pops into Mariana's office repeatedly throughout the day. He double- and triple-checks the assignment sheet to make sure there are enough staffers to set up chairs and tables after lunch. He planned the show for five o'clock so no one will be going home before. He can feel the nervous energy coursing through the clients all day. Every time he hears a behavioral outburst from somebody, Dave cringes. He says little prayers and mantras, hoping that everyone holds it together tonight.

After lunch is cleared away and the kitchen is cleaned, Dave has Carlos supervise the setup of the rec room. He doesn't want to risk putting the clients through a rehearsal, but he keeps them busy with low-stress activities. Anthony struts around all day, the very picture of self-confidence. Dave wishes he could bottle whatever gives him that.

The debs start arriving at four. They are laden with trays of cookies, table coverings, and centerpieces. Karen bustles about, directing movement with the air of a general. Dave feels her authority as a challenge to his own. He forgets that when two men, dads or husbands who got off early from work, enter dragging a substantial Christmas tree. Karen beams at Dave: "Surprise!" Dave is surprised, and delighted. A tree that tall costs a fortune in Upward Bound terms and Dave never would have spent the money. It really spruces up the room. The dads throw up a couple of strings of lights and the girls produce a bin of plastic ornaments from Target. In the time it took the Peanuts characters to turn Charlie Brown's spindly misfit tree into a beauty, the debs' tree lights up the rec room. Dave sees it as a good omen.

It's nearly showtime. Families and guests are arriving and sitting in the metal folding chairs. He sees Walter's mom and she looks nervous. Dave desperately wants to work the crowd and greet the board members, but he knows he needs to meet with his cast and give them a pre-curtain pep talk. He sees Karen chatting with the board chairman like they're old friends, so he figures they're in good hands. Dave makes his way backstage, which is an area of the rec room set off by the old accordion dividers. The cast is gathered, packed more tightly than autistic people usually like. One of the Upward Bound moms has supplied the cast with brightly colored scarves and damn if they don't look like costumes. Dave adopts a serious tone.

"Okay, guys. And gals. This is what you've been working for all this time. This is your time to shine."

Dave looks around at the faces. Some are slack and checked out, some are hyper with darting eyes. Anthony, as usual, owns the place.

Dave says, "Don't worry if you forget where you're supposed to be. Carlos will be standing right over there"—Dave points to a spot just behind the accordion divider—"and he'll remind you. Just have fun, and let's show your families what Upward Bound is all about."

Dave goes to the back of the rec room behind the audience. He's too nervous to sit. Andy sits down at the piano and starts lightly playing "O Christmas Tree" while Anthony, Drew, and Emma walk to center stage. Anthony begins to speak.

"Hi, Drew, hi, Emma. Christmas is coming and Upward Bound isn't ready for the holidays yet. Let's do something, let's put on a show."

Dave's gut clenches. Something is off. Anthony is saying the right lines, but his energy is weird. He's trying too hard to be funny. He's taken it up a thousand notches from the way he's done it in rehearsal. After he's finished his first speech, the whole cast comes out and they sing "Jingle Bells." A couple of them keep looking over to Carlos for reassurance, but otherwise it's not terrible. Walter, who's so far in the back that you can barely see him, isn't singing, but he also isn't turning in circles or making strange noises. He can see the back of Walter's mom's head as she moves around trying to get a glimpse of her son. The song ends and there are a couple of skits. Anthony continues to deteriorate. He keeps forgetting his lines, which he hasn't done in weeks. He calls out loudly to Carlos to cue him. He almost winks at the audience conspiratorially, like a *Saturday Night Live* performer who breaks character and starts cracking up. Only the audience isn't laughing with him. Dave feels bad for Anthony, but then he's not sure that Anthony realizes how badly it's going. Dave imagines that Anthony also failed to comprehend how the football team really felt about him. Anthony thought he was one of them, but he was more like a court jester. Dave didn't need to be there to know this. They had a football team at McCracken County High in Paducah, too.

It's awkward. It's uncomfortable. The friendly audience doesn't seem to mind as much as Dave does. Anthony basically throws out the script and improvises. Andy plays a few bars of Christmas songs to cover overlong silences. Dave is so busy with his frustration that he doesn't see at first what else is happening. Verbal clients like Drew join in the improvisational spirit and play along with Anthony's concoctions. It doesn't make a ton of sense, but there's more cooperation and interaction than in the rehearsed version. Suddenly the actors notice the big tree that the debs brought.

Anthony says, "Hey, guys, a tree has magically appeared."

Drew replies, "It's a Christmas miracle. It's a Christmas miracle. It's a Christmas miracle."

The cast comes forward as one and steps off the low platform that transforms the rec room into a theater. They gather around the tree as if it is the most beautiful thing they've ever seen. To be fair, beauty doesn't have a lot of competition in this place. The audience leans toward them and the tree. All except Walter. Walter has moved to the front of the platform, center stage. He stands like a statue, facing forward, away from where everyone else is looking. Dave follows his gaze and realizes that Walter is staring at his mother. Mrs. Walter is staring right back. She can finally see her son.

The time for Anthony's climactic speech has arrived. Dave holds his breath. He has no reason to believe that Anthony will remember his lines or be able to regulate his energy level. Anthony looks around at his peers and starts to speak.

"Hey, you guys, somebody did this nice thing for us. Dave, was it you?"

Dave shakes his head.

"So maybe there is an angel who wanted to bring joy to us. Sometimes it seems like angels forget about us. But we are special and we got this nice tree. I wish it was Christmas every day."

Anthony looks around as if he doesn't have any idea what to

say. Animal panic in his eyes. Thank god Andy picks it up. He launches into a loud, up-tempo "We Wish You a Merry Christmas." It seems to wake the clients up and they make a valiant effort to sing. The ones who have the motor coordination to do so, anyway. Walter is still center stage and he starts swinging his arms around. It almost looks as if he's conducting a marching band, if you have low expectations about keeping in time. The clients get excited, aware that they made it to the end. Anthony jumps up and down. Others mimic him. The group looks just a little like a clip from *Peanuts* if you squint. The singing decreases as the movement increases. Perhaps encouraged by Walter's semi-conducting, the audience starts to sing along. Some of the debutantes stand up and dance around at their seats. Dave guesses that there are cheerleaders and glee club members among them. It's a happy mess. Dave is disappointed that all his plans went out the window, but at least it was not a disaster. Andy brings the song to a big finish and the audience cheers. Anthony jumps onto the platform and bows repeatedly, the star in his glory. He almost shoves Walter over as he claims the spotlight. Mrs. Walter is once again relegated to craning her head to catch a glimpse of her son in the chaos that passes for a curtain call.

The audience and the clients move toward each other, hugging and greeting. The debs move behind the tables with their Pinterest-inspired cookie displays. They take pictures of each other for their Insta stories, their sexy poses competing with their intentionally ugly sweaters. Dave looks around for the board chairman but first sees Mrs. Walter being talked at by Karen. He joins them.

"Oh, hey, Dave, congratulations. That was so fun. Don't you love what the girls have done? It's so special that they could have this experience. It is so good for them. It's so wonderful of them to do this, right?" gushes Karen.

Dave is annoyed by Karen's deb-centered response to all his hard work. He glances at the face of Walter's mother. She looks stricken, as if Karen's oblivious comments are piercing her soul. He looks at the two women and compares them. They're about the same age, probably similar socioeconomically. Both are attractive in an early-fifties way. But Karen is snappily dressed—hair, makeup, and Botox helping along. Mrs. Walter looks tired and stressed, wearing jeans and a boxy jacket. She is staring at Karen as if she can't believe that this woman and her hothouse girls are trying to make this evening about them. Dave has always acted supportively toward his clients' families. He assumed that, by the time they land as adults in his facility, the parents have accepted the reality of their children's place in the world. One look at Walter's mom's face (what is her name?) and he suddenly realizes that the pain of exclusion never fully goes away. Walter's mom never got to see her kid onstage in elementary or high school. And this damn woman won't even let her have this much-belated night.

Dave says, "Yes, we appreciate the cookies and the tree." Turning to Mrs. Walter (he must get Mariana to look up her name, Edith probably knows it), he says, "And how about our Walter? He was terrific tonight."

Karen turns away as Mrs. Walter rearranges her face. "Yes, I couldn't believe it. It's almost like he got the audience to join in at the end." Dave assures her that he did.

The crowd swarms around the cookie tables. The debs' flashy poise is dimmed when they are forced to interact up close with the clients. Anthony valiantly tries to chat a few up but is unmoved by being shut down. Dave is pleased by the turnout. Dave has a few words with the board chairman, a local real estate developer. The guy does this because it's good for his image, Dave knows, but he takes his role seriously.

"Great show tonight, Dave old boy," he says. "I bet you're going to hit us up for more money next year."

"Actually, Brian, I've been meaning to talk to you about . . ." Dave starts. He's been waiting weeks to make an informal pitch for more funding. Brian isn't looking at Dave.

"Sorry, gotta run. The wife doesn't like me out on school nights. We'll talk soon."

And he's gone.

Dave looks at the donation baskets set up around the room. Only a few bills here and there. Dave goes up to Karen, who is chatting with another deb mom.

"Would you mind asking a few of the girls to circulate the room with the donation baskets? Who could refuse those pretty faces?"

A slight look of distaste crosses Karen's face. Dave catches it but doesn't know if it's a money thing or he was being sexist. She gets past it either way, and the girls are soon wending their way through the clumps of families, flirting and cajoling. Good call, Dave congratulates himself. Dave sees Andy sitting with a few staffers eating a pile of cute cookies.

"Andy, my man. You, sir, and your magic fingers saved the day."

"Thanks, Dave. Couldn't let the thing go off the rails."

"How'd you know you might need some extra music?"

"I had a feeling that Anthony might crack under pressure, so I brought a Christmas cheat book," Andy says.

"Good thinking. Thanks for all your hard work."

Andy nods at Dave and goes back to his conversation. Dave looks around. People are starting to leave. He cleans up a few empty tables, hoping the staffers might pick up the hint and help. Karen goes around to the debs and gives some quiet orders. The girls fan out across the room and get to work. This motivates Andy and the other staffers. A few clients and their families pitch in. Dave looks at his funny community. Camaraderie can happen in the strangest places. He is suddenly exhausted and wants to teleport himself home. He calls Carlos over and hands him a ring of keys.

"Would you mind staying and locking up? I have a spare set at home for the morning."

Dave has to show Carlos which key is which because he's

never let anyone else handle them. Dave walks to his car. Walter and his mom are right behind him.

"Good night, Dave," calls out Mrs. Walter.

Lisa, that's her name. Dave remembers now.

"Good night, folks. Walter, you're a star."

ANDY THE UNDERACHIEVER

Better sit down for this. I need to make you understand what happened today, and you are not going to like it. Do you need some water? I could make coffee. No? Okay. So. I was at work and Dave said I could back the truck up to the dumpster. We'd been clearing out a shed in that play area. I don't think anyone had been in there since before it was Upward Bound. The lock was rusted out and Dave hacked it off with a shovel. It was so musty and weird in there. So many spiderwebs. I would have just locked it back up and left it for the next guy. But Dave says he needs the storage space. Easy for him to say. He wasn't about to get dirty, so he just told us to do our best and he went back inside. Me and Chloe took old brooms and waved them around in the air. We got the massive spiderwebs off the walls and out of the center of the shed. It was so gross. I kept waiting to see some Indiana Jones treasure underneath it all, but it was just ancient lawnmowers and rakes and whatnot. Upward Bound has a couple of mow-and-blow guys who come twice a month, but I guess they must have had in-house people do the gardening at some point. Some point very long ago by the looks of things.

Chloe and I busted our butts all morning. A lot of clients didn't show up today because of the three-day weekend, and Dave didn't want to waste any staff hours, so this felt like busy work to me. You know how much I hate that. We dragged all the old stuff outside the shed. Some of it looked like it could still be usable, like metal buckets. When was the last time you saw a metal bucket, right? Chloe actually put one in her trunk without asking. She posts repurposing videos on TikTok. Anyway, we got all the junk out. There was a moldering bag of fertilizer that had been a home for rats, probably generations of rats. I know, so gross. We put on gloves and aprons, but other than old droppings, there were no signs of rats living there now.

With the shed empty, we didn't know what to do. We went inside feeling too filthy to touch anything. We washed our hands in the kitchen. We had to use that horrible-smelling powdered soap that Dave insists is as good as the more expensive stuff. The water ran brown from the filth. I had a couple of little cuts on my hands from before I put on gloves. See? It's tough to play piano with cuts on your fingers. I told you, this job is no summer camp.

Anyway, Chloe and me went to Dave and told him what we'd done. All the old rusty stuff was outside the shed in the play area. The inside of the shed was still dirty but cleared out. I thought we did pretty well, considering how bad the place was. Dave had a freak-out, though. Didn't we know that there was an activity scheduled in the play area in an hour? First of all, you might have told us. Second, there is never an actual activity in that little play yard. Dave puts it on the schedule so we can get the clients outside, so we can do cleanup in the rec room or whatever. They're adults for Chrissake, there's nothing for them to do out there but try to find some shade and wait to go back inside. Dave could have just moved them to another spot, just for today, to give us time to move the junk without killing ourselves. But nooooo. Dave tells us to load the junk into the Upward Bound pickup truck and drive it to the dumpster on the other side of the parking lot. It wasn't a long distance, but too far to walk it over one rusty piece at a time. Oh, am I up-to-date on my tetanus shots? Dave comes outside and moves the truck so that its back end is close to the little gate. Only Dave and Carlos are allowed to drive the truck.

Chloe and me have, like, a five-minute break for lunch, then it's back to it. We need a union, we should have, like, breaks, right? Isn't it against the law to make people do horrible things that aren't their job, and not even give them a break? I was annoyed, not to mention dirty and tired. I was supposed to go over to David's house tonight, but now I don't even feel like it. Anyway, it took us about a half hour to get everything in the truck and make sure nothing was left on the ground that somebody could get hurt with. I know I'm complaining a lot. Chloe had a much better attitude about it all. No, I'm not interested in Chloe. She's okay, but she's a little too gung ho for me. So she's pretty much annoying me, too, at this point. I'm getting to it, I just wanted you to feel where I was when it happened. We go inside to let Dave know it's time to move the truck to the dumpster. And how about a thank-you for getting the job done in time for the stupid activity that's not even an activity? But when we find Dave, he's giving a tour to some business-looking people and he waves us off. Like we're too filthy for outsiders. But then Dave excuses himself and comes over to us. He hands me the keys and says, "Andy, you can move the truck, just be careful." He's acting super nice for the visitors, but you can tell he's not happy to let me do it. But the activity must go on.

I get in the truck and start it. I've never actually driven anything that big. Chloe stays in the lot to direct me. I turn the truck around, everything fine so far. I put it in reverse and start backing up when Chloe suddenly screams. I think, *Oh shit*, like, I've hit her or something. I swerve, I pull the steering wheel sharp, like it's instinct. Then I hear the crunch. I've run into a car parked in the parking lot. No, it wasn't mine. It would have been less bad if I had hit my own stupid car. No offense. Then I see this client, Jorge—I've told you about Jorge, you just don't remember—streaking across the parking lot. He does this running thing all the time but it's scary. I guess I could have hit him if Chloe hadn't screamed. The car I hit instead had a big scrunch in it. I'm sick to my stomach. Then I realize the car is Dave's. I know. He drives an old Honda Civic, but still. Carlos came out and got Jorge. Dave entered the scene right after. I assumed he'd be really mad, but he was, like, sad. Like this is exactly what he expected when he gave me the keys. That made me feel worse than yelling. We still had to unload the junk from the truck. Dave says his car is still drivable and goes inside to call the insurance company. He thinks the place's insurance will probably pay for the repairs to his car, but he may not want to make a claim. The board would hear that he let me drive the truck. It might still end up falling on us, on our insurance. I'm so sorry. I was just following orders. What was I supposed to do? Hit Jorge?

No, Dave didn't fire me. He needs me. But I feel bad. Is there anything for dinner? I'm starved.

WALTER AND EMMA
DO CHITCHAT

Walter arrives at Upward Bound at eight-thirty. His mom has to be at work at nine. Mom signs him in and has a little chitchat with Edith at the front desk. Mom often brags about him to people, even strangers, but Walter is envious of her ability to talk to anyone. He doesn't know if she was always like this, or if she developed the skill after she realized that he was never going to hold up his end of the conversation. Before Dad died, the two of them had chattered constantly. Walter was always amazed by how much they found to talk about. He listened to them closely, although most people would assume from Walter's behavior that he was tuned out. They talked about current news and Dad's job. Dad would tell stories about things going on at work and use too much detail for Mom, but she knew that he needed to sound everything out. These conversations involved the nuts and bolts of TV production, which can get boring, but Dad could get worked up about them. She usually gave her impressions of the situation and would tuck a bit of advice into her comments. Mom just talked about me and my day. Their chat was incessant and they made each other laugh all the time. He could hear them at night belly-laughing at something through the walls.

Since Dad passed, Walter worries that Mom doesn't have anyone to talk to. Not strictly true. Since the day that he was three, when she realized that he was not mentally retarded, as she had been told by doctors, she has kept up a one-sided conversation with him. She talks to him as if he could answer back. Walter has always appreciated this. He responds to her in his head, which almost seems like a conversation, at least to him. Sometimes an echolalic script comes out of his mouth—irrelevant, unbidden, unwelcome. People who don't get it try to respond to the echolalia. Not Mom. She just says something else, and the conversation continues. He is aware that it's not fair to her, so he tries to be patient when she goes on chatting with Edith. She's going to be late for work at this point. Walter walks back toward the rec room without saying goodbye to his mother. He only performs greetings when prompted to do so, and the one who prompts is still conversing with the receptionist.

Walter walks into the rec room and stands there. He is one of the few Upward Bound clients who does not get there on a short bus. The buses don't arrive until nine, so Walter is often the first one here. He doesn't mind, because he likes the quiet, but he wishes that someone would leave out a puzzle or book so he didn't get so bored waiting. Dave keeps everything locked up tight. Walter is standing near the window, watching the light flickering off the pool as if the window were a video screen. He is surprised when Emma enters. She usually arrives on the third bus around 9:05. It's only 8:39. Something must have been different in Emma's house today. Maybe she missed the bus and it took her parent less time to get there even so. He would ask her, but there's no way his mouth could form the question. Even if he managed it, she couldn't answer. She makes tiny little sounds, like little breathy bird sounds, instead of words. Walter is left to conjecture as to why Emma is early today.

Emma comes over to the window and looks out, as if to see what Walter is staring at. The sunlight flaming off the pool and fractured by the window draws her gaze as well. He wonders if it appears the same to her as it does to him. They say that no two people experience autism the same way. How would anyone know what was happening in their heads? Maybe Emma and Walter have exactly the same hallucinogenic visual response to the sun on the water refracted through the glass window. As they stand in the shabby rec room, Walter realizes that he will never know.

Walter is aware that Emma can also point to letters to communicate, like he can. Like most spellers, they need communication partners or aides to facilitate their pointing. There is no such trained aide at Upward Bound. Their skills are dormant here. Whatever conversation Walter and Emma might have with actual words requires two other people present. They have conversed this way over the years, but it was stilted and unsatisfying to Walter. He prefers this, just the two of them, letting their energies do the talking.

Walter and Emma learned to point as kids, taught by the same amazing lady. They met at age six playing in a McDonald's play place while their mothers chatted and realized that they had something in common. It's almost twenty years later, and their moms are still friends. Walter and Emma were both able to point at letters to get through school, and they both attended college before they both ended up at Upward Bound. Emma went to a small Christian college where they were loving and tolerant of her, but Emma was nonetheless overwhelmed with anxiety and has yet to finish her degree. She needed a break, and her mom sent her to Upward Bound, thinking it would be okay since Walter was there.

Walter learned all this by listening to the two mothers talking at the occasional meetups of nonspeaking spellers that Emma's mom organized. Walter and Emma have known each other for so long, and he considers them friends. He knows they're friends. They may even love each other a little. Being friends without speaking requires faith. Not the Christian kind of faith, which Emma clings to but Walter does not. The faith that allows you to believe that your friend feels for you what you feel for them. Even when you can't show it or speak of it.

Walter feels Emma's anxiety lurking below her placid demeanor. It's like a painful electrical current submerged in mud. Everyone thinks Emma is so calm, but Walter knows that it's because of the disconnect between her emotions and her face.

Nervous and upset can be confused with happy and calm if you don't stand quietly next to her and hear the thrumming of her wires. That's what Walter does in the moments that they're looking out the window. He listens with all his heart.

Walter is pretty sure that Emma is also listening to him. He can feel her energy trying to find its way into his. He wonders what his sounds like to her. Maybe she hears in colors, maybe she sees with music. By the time the first short bus disgorges its passengers at 8:58, Walter feels as if he has had a twenty-year running conversation with his friend, with belly laughs and chitchat. Walter thinks that he hears Emma saying that she cherishes him.

CAMP CAMMIE

First came the camp counselor. I was sitting on the floor of my cabin. My duffel bag was open in front of me. It wasn't my duffel bag, actually. It was my dad's. He lent it to me for this five-day adult sleepaway camp for people with disabilities. This was my first time being away from home overnight. I had survived the first two nights, but they hadn't gone so well. No one seemed very pleased with me so far. I was going through the bag, hoping that Mom might have hidden a train or some gummies in there. Something that would make this strange place feel friendlier. My fingers landed on a long, thin plastic container with seven little compartments. I have these. My mom uses them to organize the fistful of medications and supplements I take every day. But the one I just found in the bag was Dad's. It had two days' worth of pills in it. He was on a five-day trip recently and he obviously forgot to take out the container.

Dad was a pretty important executive for a TV company. He was the guy in charge of the production facts. May I say that he was very good at his job, but he was not as great at finding the balance at home. My mom was not willing to be ordered about like an underling, and Dad didn't have an eye for domestic details. Mom would never have neglected to remove a pill container from her luggage, much less let me take it to camp. But there I was.

I was holding it in my hand when the counselor came in looking for me. I was late for breakfast. The counselor was already annoyed about having to walk all the way to the cabins to retrieve me, the new camper who wasn't yet with the program. His eyes got large when he saw the pill holder in my hand. There are no pills in the cabins. There are two nurses on staff here. They dispense everyone's pills at mealtimes. Everyone here is on some kind of medication, so they take it very seriously. The counselor rushed over to me and grabbed the pill container out of my hand. He looked at it and his demeanor changed to one of panic. *Oh my god!* he kept saying. *Did you take all these?* He yanked me to my feet and forced my mouth open, as if to catch some errant capsule dancing down my throat. He then took me by the arm and pulled me up the path to the main building.

In my head, I am firmly but calmly explaining the circumstances to the counselor, whose name I haven't learned yet. Dad's bag, Dad's pills, can you keep them safe until he comes to pick me up at the end of the week? But of course, my mouth doesn't work that way. The only word I could summon from my voice was "Henry." Henry is number three of Thomas the Tank Engine's friends. Henry always arrives just in time to save the day. When I am pushed too far, when I am stressed beyond a quick recovery, I call out to Henry, loudly, repeatedly, in a high-pitched voice. Please, someone, come to my rescue. A twenty-two-year-old man crying out "Henry" over and over unnerves many people, this camp counselor among them. We were both in a heightened state when the young man pulled me into the nurses' office.

Both nurses were in the dining hall distributing meds. The counselor used his phone to alert someone that there was a possible overdose in progress. If I had more control over my facial muscles, I would be rolling my eyes. By the time the nurses rushed in, I was doing my best to appear alert and unimpaired. I was hungry, too. The head person of the camp hurried in. She was a brittle blond lady who had her favorites. My mother had already alienated herself, and me by association, by being too needy about my diet, my EpiPen, my allergies, my meds. I had perseverated on "Mom and Dad" since the moment they left, repeating those three words over and over, so everyone on the premises was exasperated with me, counselors and campers alike. I knew it but couldn't stop. I didn't like it there, and all I wanted was for the experiment to be over. The way that the head lady and the nurses were dealing with this crisis, I got the distinct impression that they were happy to have an excuse to get rid of me early.

Head lady left the nurses' office to call my parents. I don't know what she said to them or how she characterized the incident. Once she was gone, the younger nurse returned to the dining hall to finish doling out pills to campers who weren't in nurse prison. The older nurse, obviously perturbed, did a perfunctory examination of me. She took my pulse and checked my pupils. I'm pretty sure they knew I hadn't taken anything horrible. They were following a policy that had the added benefit of ridding themselves of me. Right back atcha, Camp Cammie.

Camp Cammie is the mountain retreat owned and operated by Upward Bound. Most weeks are reserved for disabled kids, but they open the camp experience to disabled adults for one or two weeks over the summer. My parents didn't send me here as a kid. I guess they didn't think I was up to it. By age twenty-two, even they thought it was time for some independence and a camping experience. I was not convinced, but I typed "yes" when Mom showed me the brochure. I was torn about being vindicated. Even in this environment, I was the only nonspeaking autistic person. No aide to help me with the letter board that would have allowed me to clear up the pill container situation before it escalated to Defcon 1. Now there was trouble.

Camp Cammie is supposed to be a haven for disabled people, a place where everyone can enjoy nature and community no matter what their limitations. Yet here I was, incarcerated, unable to explain or defend myself, punished for something I didn't do. I expect this level of injustice from the typical world: educators, medical personnel, law enforcement, people at large. I've encountered the willful bias against nonspeakers my entire life. I didn't expect to be rejected by Camp Cammie. Yet rejected I was. Forcibly evicted. I had been in the nurses' office less than half an hour when some counselor—I had yet to learn anyone's name, that's how connected I was to this warm camping community—dumped my/Dad's duffel bag inside the door, packed but not neatly.

I learned that my parents would be there any minute to pick me up. We lived several hours from Camp Cammie. They had taken advantage of this rare me-free week to have a getaway of their own. Coincidentally, they were at a lodge nearby. They arrived at Camp Cammie so soon that I barely had time to be concerned about my mother's reaction to this turn of events. I didn't worry about my dad; it's different with him. But Mom deserved the break this week was supposed to give her. I wouldn't blame her for being disappointed. I was disappointed for her. Not for myself, of course. I hated the place and couldn't wait to get out of there. But she needed a break from being my person, and who wouldn't.

Suddenly my mother entered the room like a virago. I was afraid of her; I can only imagine what the camp people thought. Her first action was to march over to me, look me over closely, and give me a brief, fierce hug. I knew then that someone other than me was in her crosshairs. Mother turned to the nurse and demanded to see the pill container. She cried out that she had been right, what she had said on the phone. She proceeded to go through all the observations and explanations that I would have made if I were blessed with the gift of speech.

Dad's bag. Dad's pills. Dad's recent five-day trip. Common sense would tell you that I hadn't taken anything harmful. The only prescription drug in the container was a Metformin for Dad's blood pressure. The rest of the pills were fish oil and saw palmetto, for god's sake. And by the way, Walter is not an idiot and wouldn't have taken someone else's pills. And you're treating him like a goddamned criminal. By this time, brittle-head lady had entered. Mom delivered her righteous indignation directly at her. She wanted the lady to admit that they had overreacted, but brittle lady stood firm right back. Mom said that brittle lady should be ashamed of herself. Her job was to give Walter a camp experience. Mom guessed that I had been scripting a lot and annoying people. Yeah, welcome to Walter's disability, she practically screamed in brittle lady's face.

Dad had hung back and let Mom do her thing, but now he picked up his/my bag and said to me that it was time to go. Mom followed us but turned to lob one more ball of mother fire at the lady. Be better than this. With a look that should have turned the lady into brittle stone, Mom got in the car with me and Dad, slamming the door behind her. We started the long drive down the mountain in silence. Mom's anger shimmered off her in little sparks. She repeated all the injustice and intolerance Camp Cammie had committed. Her voice became sad and plaintive toward the end. She said the hard thing out loud. If Camp Cammie wouldn't tolerate me, who would?

Dad stopped at McDonald's to get us breakfast. We never talked about Camp Cammie after that.

CARLOS THE CAMARADERIE COUNSELOR

Carlos made one last sweep across the room. Everyone was seated, all had a bowl, the noise level was tolerable. Breakfast in the books. As he turned to move on to his next task, he spied with his camera eye a picture of despair. You could reasonably argue that the entire vista currently facing him qualified as a catastrophe of inhuman proportions. Twenty-eight disabled adults whose lives were being spent in shabby boredom represented to Carlos the wastage of twenty-eight glorious galaxies. He imagined his people as swirling masses of light and potential. Their existence dwelled in an off-world space, which is why people on Earth disregard them. Carlos wasn't thinking of these grand, silent tragedies this morning. He was concerned about one bent head only.

Jorge sat slumped in his usual spot, the back table, the farthest from the door. In the beginning, before Carlos knew anything about anything, he had assumed things about Jorge. This was six years ago, not long after graduation. Jorge's massive size reminded Carlos of a guy he knew at Rosemead High. The guy was a beast on the football field, but he was a terrible bully in the offseason, when he didn't have a school-sanctioned outlet for his chaos. Carlos watched Jorge like a hawk his first couple of days at Upward Bound, waiting for the giant to blow. Carlos's wary eye could be traced back to his childhood days in El Monte, where he had to watch his back inside his mother's apartment as well as outside it. When Carlos looked closer at Jorge, when he ventured to peer under the heavy lids, he saw that Jorge was not a powder keg but a pillow.

After that, Carlos still kept an eye on Jorge, but it was more to figure him out. Carlos had no background in disability things. His sister got him the job after she'd been working at Upward Bound a long time. If she ever talked about the people there, he sure as hell didn't listen. Now that he was hanging out with them all day, he was curious. Some clients obviously needed to be there. They were in a wheelchair or their bodies were super spastic. Some were straight-up retarded. But there were others, and Carlos would even say most of them, that seemed like they could be somewhere else. Doing something. Jorge remained a mystery to Carlos at first. He hovered between the two camps, and Carlos found that he really wanted to know if anyone was home in there. Carlos started arranging to be with Jorge when the clients were split into small groups for an activity. Jorge didn't participate in anything actively. Carlos couldn't tell if he wouldn't or if he couldn't.

*

Jorge never spoke. Carlos assumed at first that this was a choice. A fuck you to a system that never listened anyway. As he spent more time in Jorge's presence, when he was adjacent to the bubble surrounding Jorge, he could hear little snuffling grunts that did not sound like speech would be coming. Carlos got this. Many of the clients here didn't talk or talked in nonsense. There was one day, about a month after he started working at Upward Bound. Carlos was watching the clients as they milled around in the lame-ass little park across the street from the place. Jorge sat in a tiny spot of shade under the little kids' play structure. He looked like a giant egg nesting in wood chips and fiberglass. Carlos wasn't obligated, but he crossed the hot playground and crouched down very low so that he could see what Jorge was up to. Down to, more accurately.

Jorge was in deep concentration. Carlos tried to figure out what he could possibly be focused on. Carlos silently looked at the ground where Jorge's deep gaze had landed. He looked intently and was at first amazed to see that the wood chips had a million other things mixed in. Details became clearer as his eyes adjusted to the close-up view. There were many little specks of things—a bit of plastic bag, dirt, and sand—but one discernible object. There lay at a sad angle a tiny plastic arm with a little hand on one end and a plug on the other. Carlos didn't have a ton of toys growing up, but he knew what this was. The arm from a Mr. Potato Head. Carlos thought of the kid whose Potato Head would now be a one-armed bandit. Carlos then peered hard at Jorge, confirming that it was the arm that held Jorge's attention. There was a look of longing on Jorge's normally impassive face. Why didn't he just pick it up? He wanted to so clearly, but it was as if the object were miles away and inaccessible. Carlos was still alert to triggering Jorge, so he said as quietly as he could, "Arm." Carlos waited. He thought that if Jorge could talk at all, maybe he would repeat the word. Carlos could hear a little aspiration of air and sound. Maybe it meant arm, maybe it meant yes, maybe it was just breathing. Carlos waited. It occurred to him that maybe the act of picking up something you really wanted was as impossible for Jorge as talking. It's not that he didn't want to, it's that he couldn't. Maybe he needed help.

"Do you want to pick it up?" asked Carlos in the calmest voice he could muster.

Breath with a little sound meant yes. Carlos slowly picked up his own hand, like to model picking it up, but Jorge's hands stayed in his lap. Carlos didn't want to just do it for him. That's what everybody did. Carlos reached over and tapped Jorge's right hand.

"Use this one," he said more firmly.

That seemed to wake up Jorge's body and he suddenly snatched the little arm. He held it in his hand. Carlos saw Jorge's big round body relax as he raised his head. He didn't look at the source of his salvation—he looked away from Carlos. But Carlos could sense that he'd done something for the guy. It was a decent feeling. As the play session in the park ended, Carlos stood and held his hand out to Jorge to help him hoist that big body upward. Jorge didn't take his hand, didn't seem to notice it. He rolled to his side and sort of rose from all fours, horribly awkwardly. Carlos felt like he'd been left hanging after offering a sincere high-five. His pride got bruised. He walked at the back of the pack as the clients crossed the street toward their scummy building. Carlos sulked for the rest of the day. He couldn't figure out how he wanted to be, who he wanted to be, for however long he worked here. He was sure it wouldn't be long. He couldn't be all girly enthusiasm like the white girl whose name he hadn't learned yet. She clearly believed she was saving lives here. But being cool and standing back, observing more than participating, the stance that got him through Rosemead in one piece, didn't work here. You couldn't actually perform the job that way, and it mostly made you look like an asshole.

Carlos looked around at the other people who worked there. Everyone in the same stupid T-shirt. He almost didn't agree to take the job because of the stupid T-shirt, but he figured Mariana might kick him out if he didn't do something, and this was being handed to him. He didn't like that, either, but he had made an effort to find a job in the neighborhood and no one was interested in what he had to offer. Carlos knew that he may not have presented himself in the most employable light. He bristled at the lectures at school about how to dress for a job interview. They sounded like the nagging, sugary voice of Mariana trying to dress him up for church when he was a kid. Now he was wearing a purple T-shirt thanks to Mariana. She always won in the end. He smirked to himself because he knew that her influence on him had a shelf life. As soon as he built up a little time in this job to show he could, he'd get a better job and move out. In the meantime, he needed a mask or costume that he could put on while he was there, just to get through it without going nuts.

Carlos watched the other staffers but saw no role models. Dave was a joke, of course, but he knew how to do the administrative stuff so he wasn't entirely useless. The other staffers were either too young or too stupid to teach Carlos anything. Andy was almost cool, but he seemed more interested in the girl staffers than the clients. Andy was white and he was a dude, which set him apart. He was going to the community college but didn't appear to have much going on. He wasn't a jerk or an idiot. Carlos and Andy were both twenty when they started at Upward Bound a few months apart. While Andy might have the white privilege thing going for him, Carlos saw his own ambition as superior. They met in the middle and might even become friends. Other staffers were the white girl with too much caring, and a nice, quiet girl who was mixed. There were part-timers who came and went, but the four of them were the full-time regulars. At least until next week, because the quiet girl was leaving. Apparently that happened a lot and apparently the jobs were hard to fill, so the ones left behind had to carry the weight. Carlos thought about the day when he'd be the one leaving the hole. If he didn't get out soon, he'd end up having seniority.

Carlos looked up and saw Mariana standing near the door. She was speaking to the manager of the building and pointing up to some flickering fluorescent lights. The OG kind that are six feet long and will gradually drive you apeshit. Carlos often forgot to look at Mariana for long stretches. If he were to catch her eye, she might recall some chore or point of instruction. Here at work, he observed her from a distance. She was not his supervisor, Dave was. Carlos saw how smart and competent Mariana looked as she dealt with the older building manager. She remained calm and sweet with the man, even when he was trying to give her some story, and she held her ground. After finishing her business with the manager, Mariana sat at one of the tables and spent a few minutes chatting with clients. That wasn't her job—she was strictly an administrative aide. But her pretty face and kind eyes brightened every person at the table.

Carlos suddenly laughed a little snort. The best thing this place had going for it was his sister. Of course it was. Carlos realized that Mariana held the key to his survival here. Not because she would get him out of a jam if he screwed up. She probably would, she always had. But because her natural temperament was perfect for this environment. She was nice, but not fake or gushy. Mariana always held a little something back. Carlos held just about everything back, but maybe here it's better to let out a little line. Just enough so that the clients didn't think you hated it here. It's not their fault they're here. If he could keep them from feeling worse about being here by acting a little more like Mariana, that would be good for everyone, including him.

*

Carlos briefly recalled those early days at Upward Bound as he stood, hands on hips, wondering what was up with Jorge. Six years they'd shared space. Carlos felt like he knew Jorge better than he knew anyone else outside his family. But he couldn't explain that to anyone. There was this kind of Vulcan mind meld that had blossomed slowly between them. Managing work tasks became secondary to Carlos. His main concern was angling to be in Jorge's space. When he was within arm's length of Jorge, Carlos swore he could tell what the big guy was feeling: hot or cold, interested or bored, calm or anxious. At first he didn't give the physical impressions any credence. One time, Carlos got the strongest feeling of hunger, and without thinking he said out loud to Jorge, "Lunch is in twenty minutes, buddy. You gonna be able to make it?" Jorge had this weird response that made Carlos think of a basketball being suddenly but only slightly deflated. An awareness came over Carlos that hunger was indeed the issue right then for Jorge, but knowing lunch was that soon put him at ease. Carlos learned to trust those impressions. Carlos and Jorge communicated better in that other space than Carlos did with anyone else out loud, including

Mariana. He had no tangible proof, but he was pretty sure that Jorge saw or felt his stuff, too.

The mind meld had been operational now for about three years. Carlos had never mentioned it to a soul. The curse of it was that Jorge had a lot of pain—deep, real, hard-won pain—that Carlos absorbed through the skin. Some nights he went home and felt paralyzed with muscle soreness. Carlos had gathered basic facts about Jorge. He had lingered in Mariana's office one day for the purpose of sneaking a look at Jorge's file. This was very much against regulation. If Dave had a stick up his butt about anything, and he had several, the biggest stick was privacy. Carlos got it, these people were vulnerable. Maybe the clients wouldn't want their diagnoses or living situations to be openly aired. Although it's not as if any of the clients here could pass for normal. But privacy can be taken too far. Dave won't let anyone take pictures. For young people right now, it's like telling them not to breathe.

Jorge's address was L.A., but the neighborhood was East Garvey, Carlos could tell by the street. He was pretty sure it was a group home, so there's no telling where the family lives. Carlos isn't quite sure how involved the family is. The emergency contact on Jorge's file is a social worker. That could mean a lot of things. Jorge is an adult and his family is not responsible as if he were still a child. He could be part of a loving clan of people who work to survive and lack the resources to take care of him. He could be abandoned. Carlos's Spidey sense told him that abandonment was a part of Jorge's makeup. It took Carlos a surprisingly long time to realize that this hole is what bound them. Carlos thought so infrequently of his birth mother that he often forgot that she had chosen drugs and booze over him. Over Mariana, too, he imagined, although Mariana took such great pains to appear well brought up that even he was persuaded. Carlos and Jorge both understood what it was to not have a mama bird and a proper nest.

All Carlos learned from Jorge's file was that docile Jorge did not have much of a bureaucratic footprint. So be it. Many people live off the grid for ideological reasons. Other people were not given access to the grid to begin with, as if their entire existence wasn't worth a line of data entry, much less a Gmail account. No one had ever bothered to set Jorge up with any digital identity, apart from the administration of his blunt-force services: SSI, group home with supervision, forty hours of Upward Bound per week. No text account, no phone, of course. Who would he talk to? Carlos had this awareness. He might be the only person in Jorge's daily life who honestly had affection for him, who saw him and even knew him a little.

Many months of SSI payments were invisibly processed on Jorge's behalf as he and Carlos developed and embellished their unlikely, otherworldly camaraderie. Carlos not only bore the brunt of Jorge's unspoken pain, but he wore the weight like the mantle of a chieftain. It gave him authority. Not authority over the clients or the other staffers, but over his own bad self. He needed to stay calm and patient to make Jorge's day go smoothly. He needed to stay vigilant to guard against Jorge's tendency to elope, which Carlos thought was a hysterical term for a disabled person who runs away. Couples who elope are running toward something—perhaps Jorge is, too.

*

Carlos strolled across the rec room and kneeled next to Jorge. Only from the floor did he have any hope of glimpsing Jorge's face. Carlos made sure not to touch Jorge, who could sometimes be prickly about that, even with him. Carlos entered his camaraderie field and listened. He didn't look at him but stared at the floor as Jorge did. There was no toy arm to point the way today. Carlos listened as a wave of suffering came over him and it almost made him crumple to the floor.

"Oh man," he said quietly. "I'm so sorry."

As Carlos stayed in that position of piety, he saw the floor for exactly what it was. The aging linoleum that was neither gray nor brown. The remaining flecks of seventies design. The rubber tip on the bottom of a metal folding chair. The bottom. Jorge was at the bottom of a well so deep that Carlos wasn't sure he could even call down to him. Carlos just stayed where he was.

*

Carlos did not exercise self-possession growing up. His mother had gone to prison when Carlos was six and Mariana was sixteen. Their mother had not been much of a mother before that, so it wasn't a big change for little Carlos. He accepted Mariana in the role of mother because that was always her role. That also meant straining at the harness that she tried to use to rein him in. She encouraged him to do homework alongside her doing hers, but it was boring. She gave him little chores to do, but he didn't bother. He knew that if he didn't empty the trash, she would eventually do it herself. She begged him to let her know where he was going and when he'd be back, but he'd save up a cutting "You're not my mother" for such occasions. Carlos considered himself a free agent, and he wasn't about to let his straight-arrow, Miss Perfect sister boss him around.

Carlos came home one night earlier than usual. He found Mariana on the kitchen floor with her head resting on a chair, fast asleep. Her face and hair melted onto the chair seat. She was the very picture of exhaustion and despair. Bills were stacked neatly on the small table above her head next to her books from school. She had graduated high school by then and was going to the closest state college. The dishes were half done. It was as if she had just collapsed from the weight of her chores. Carlos stood there for several beats. He had never seen his sister like this. She always juggled everything with a simpy smile on her face, never letting on that she bore someone else's burden. He thought about helping her to her room, but he hated to wake her. She'd probably nag at him about something. She looked surprisingly comfortable down there. He stepped carefully over her, grabbed a box of Froot Loops, and retreated to his room.

*

Carlos didn't move from his spot on the floor even after his legs started to cramp. Breakfast was over and he was grateful to Andy for getting the clients together for morning announcements. The morning meeting routine used to include a song and the Pledge of Allegiance, but when Carlos first started being assigned to lead it, like four years ago, he refused to do the baby stuff. He just pulled up a chair and talked about whatever was going on that day. It wasn't long before the other staffers picked up on the improvement. Dave's coffee hour prevented him from learning that one of his protocols had been hammered out until it was too late. Dave seemed to be just a little afraid of Carlos, and this gave him the ability to tweak regulations into more functional shapes.

Carlos barely registered it when Andy called out, "Hey, everybody, welcome to your Thursday." Chairs scuffled, bodies shifted, but Carlos and Jorge remained still. An idea was making its way from Jorge's brain to the calcified circuits that regulated, or rather dysregulated, his big body, and Carlos picked the gist of it out of the narrow space between them. Jorge was in a greater state of despair and anxiety than usual. Carlos couldn't comfort him with his presence alone. A more powerful totem, a comfort item to ritualize upon, was being demanded. Carlos heard the need more loudly than Andy's congenial voice. Carlos knew, as most of them did, that Jorge was attached to Mr. Potato Head. The why of it meant nothing. Can anyone say why they love their comfort item, truthfully?

*

Carlos had an item. Mariana didn't even know about it, and their apartment was small. Mariana made his bed every morning because she needed it made for her own reasons. But she overlooked the little ceramic thimble that was always behind the leg of his bed right under where his pillow was. It wasn't like a functional thimble, one that someone who actually sews would use. It was the souvenir kind that they sell in gift stores next to the collectible spoons. It was white with a tiny little picture that was meant to be Sedona. The picture, small and orange, and the name always gave him a little lift. He'd never been there, of course. Road trips with the family did not happen. But one day, on an outing to the thrift store with his mom and Mariana, he must have been four or so, he had spotted the little ceramic bit by the cash register where they keep the stuff that's easy to steal. It was in his scale, small and insignificant, but with the fuzziest hint of adventure. He knew better than to ask for a toy, but maybe his mom would think differently about something like this. It was almost useful. His mom was buying clothes, and when little Carlos held up the ceramic thimble, the lady said, "Ten cents." His mom may have hesitated for a beat, but his face must have been sweet enough to cause her to shrug and let him keep it.

Mariana was fourteen and was looking at the books. She

brought up a book to maybe buy, but Mom said no. Mariana hadn't seen the thimble purchase so she didn't even know how unfair it was. She just put the book back. Carlos was too little to feel guilty about getting something special when his sister was denied. Mostly he felt happy to have the smooth, hard, small thing concealed in his hand, which he kept in his pocket until they got home. He liked rubbing his tiny fingers over the pebbled surface of the porcelain. Sometimes he used it as a vessel. He would put water in it and drink it while playing soldier or policeman, like it was his canteen. He would fill it with dirt and empty it into a toy truck like it was a workman's bucket.

It wasn't until his mother was long gone that he realized it was the last thing she gave him. That wasn't why he always knew where it was, either in his pocket or behind his bed. It could comfort him when he fussed with it, when he rolled it around his fingers. He would stick it on the end of his finger and tap it on the bedstand gently. As he got older, he left it behind his bed more and in his pocket less. He often draped his arm over the side of the bed and held the little thing as he went to sleep. As a teenager he was embarrassed by his connection to his object. Seemed like dependence to him, and he wasn't anyone's dependent. But since working at Upward Bound, especially since getting to know Jorge, Carlos had become aware that everyone has needs, and that being tolerant can be applied to oneself.

*

Dangerous things can happen when a person is deprived of comfort. Every time a comfort item is yanked from you is like a death. It's cruel and unnecessary. Upward Bound, that is, Dave, thought that clients would be more engaged in activities if their hands were liberated of their juvenile obsessions. There were only a few clients for whom that edict was tragically misguided. Emma was most able to participate when holding two plastic spoons. How can we judge that? What right does anyone have to take control over an adult woman's autonomy? Carlos always gave Emma her spoons and Dave never noticed. Dave was not very observant of the clients' bodies, only their compliance.

Jorge was well known for his comfort item. Mr. Potato Head was the only thing that could soothe the buried beast within him. He made the free-time activity hour the center of his day, conserving his resources prior to one-thirty and checking out of his body at two-thirty until the buses arrived. Most clients spent that undirected hour doing a puzzle or game or sitting and waiting to be directed again. Jorge went straight for the closet where the preschool toys were kept, the only time it was opened during the day, and roughly but lovingly took out the disintegrating cardboard box containing Mr. Potato Head. He sat down and put the arms and legs in the right holes and always used the classic bowler hat and moustache as pictured on the box. Then the toy sat cradled in Jorge's big hands. He did nothing, but his head was at a neutral angle for this brief interlude, whereas it was concave for the rest of the hours. When Carlos mastered his listening skills, he heard Jorge's heart rate go down at the completion of Mr. P's body parts. Carlos didn't get it, but he did. He always made sure he had the keys to the closet in hand and was standing at the closet when the clock said one-thirty. It was one thing Jorge could count on. Carlos couldn't do much for his friend-slash-client, but he could give him one bright moment of certainty in his slog of a day.

*

While Andy carried on with the morning announcements, Carlos remained kneeling in front of Jorge, listening. Basal temp was high, anxiety an eleven out of ten. Carlos's listening skills often had a calming effect on Jorge, but today the silent giant was immune to Carlos's compassionate brain energy. Carlos heard the need for Mr. P so loudly that it was as if there was real screaming. But it was only 9:20, and not unlocking the toy closet until free hour was one of the few of Dave's rules he actually agreed with. Carlos struggled, but only briefly. Now that Dave had finally trusted him with a set of keys, he felt deputized to make the difficult calls when a client's well-being was at stake. Jorge was about to blow, he knew, and desperate times call for drastic measures.

As stealthily as he could, Carlos removed the busy keychain from his pocket, giving Jorge a tiny glimpse so that there was no misunderstanding of his intention. He slowly stood up and realized that the clients were all facing the toy closet in their morning meeting positions. But Andy was wrapping up, and if Carlos timed it right he could slip in and grab Mr. P while the clients transitioned to their first activity. Andy finished his spiel and directed the clients to the patio for a crossword finder activity. Milling and slow-moving, the clients' forward motion was impeded by the placement of Tom's wheelchair in front of the door to the patio. Carlos moved to the closet and kept his back to the others, but Jorge was bearing down on him. Jorge jostled Carlos just as he was plucking the closet key from the jingly nest in his palm, and the keys dropped to the floor. The noise was dulled by the old linoleum, but it was enough to get Drew's attention.

"No closet 'til free time. No closet 'til free time." Drew could go on for hours once stuck.

Carlos scooped up the keys and managed to get the correct one lined up, but it was too late. Carlos forged ahead anyway. Bad decision, he knew, but Jorge was hovering so close behind him that he hoped the big guy would provide some cover. He got the closet open, but Jorge bruised into him trying to get at his prized pal. Carlos dropped the keys again and bent down to retrieve them. In that split second, Jorge lunged over him and grabbed Mr. P's box with his giant paw. His elopement was like lightning charging the room with an unearthly halo of bad omen. By the time Carlos had straightened up, Jorge was gone, having flung open the closet door in his flight. The clients moved in to see what was happening and Anthony called out, "Cowabunga, dude!"

Carlos struggled through the bodies but Jorge wasn't in sight. Carlos burst through the rec room door and saw Walter standing in the hall staring at the front door as if he were a signpost. Carlos ran through some late bus arrivals at the front door and saw Jorge crossing the street toward the park. It was a moderately busy street and there was no crosswalk, but Jorge plodded along. It was a miracle no one hit him. Before Carlos could catch up, a police car passed and turned around, ready to question the jaywalker. Carlos had a bad sense, as a young man of color confronting law enforcement. He had to wait for cars to go past. He watched helplessly as the cops exited their vehicle and approached Jorge, who crouched egg-like in the parking lot, Mr. P clutched protectively in his hands. Carlos finally broke across the street, yelling, "It's okay, I've got him!" But the cops were on alert for whatever they thought Jorge might be capable of. Carlos had a tiny flash of his own first impression of his gentle friend.

Carlos was driven by something greater than love to reach Jorge's side. His only thought was to protect Jorge from his panicked and chaotic body. He got to him and started to bend down as a familiar, consoling shield. Carlos glanced up and was shocked to see that the cops looked angry and had their guns out. The absurdity almost made him laugh, but just at that moment, Jorge lost it. Mr. P went flying as pops rang out. Shock overtook Carlos's forward propulsion. His body numbed, his mind relaxed. He collapsed across Jorge's back and shoulders, forever his angel. Then, brief waking moments with a veil of gauze lifting from his impressions. Jorge being taken by a black-clad figure. No, no, stop. A crush of men, hovering, touching, lifting. *Thunk*, metallic, bumpy. Love, his sister's gentle face. Mariana, my dearest Mariana.

AVERY THE TEAM MEMBER

The father calls out to his screaming son, "Can't you hold on for five fucking seconds, I'm on the phone here." The bearded man stands in the women's accessories area while his child stomps noisily. Avery can see and hear them from her register. She pulls the long sleeves of her red T-shirt over the blue finger-shaped shadows lingering on her forearms. She hates the customers who stay glued to their phones while they shop. They make the stupidest mistakes at checkout. Like leaving behind their wallets or half their items. Avery doesn't care about the abandoned credit card or forgotten Lysol. She worries about the little kids staring at the wrong side of the device devouring their parents' focus and attention. She's no expert, but Avery assumes that most kids would escalate their behaviors to compete with the powerful computer in their parent's face. As in the scene playing out in front of her.

Avery is pulled back to her duties when a tired young mom starts piling diapers and brightly colored packets of toddler snack food on her conveyor belt. The job of unloading her cart is challenged by the toddler herself, who takes the items off the belt and puts them in her mouth. Avery doubts she is going to get Covid from baby spit, but she doesn't love scanning items that have come via mouth. Mom's hands fly as she juggles purchases and payments. Avery notices that the mom manages to grip her phone while performing the tasks of many hands. Avery completes the sale after judging the mom for dipping her card instead of tapping it. The bearded man and his kid have moved on, but Avery can still hear the guy.

Avery leans against the back of her checkout stand and breathes deep intentional yoga breaths. She has begun doing yoga classes on YouTube. The breathing part is really important, but she keeps forgetting to pay attention to it. Now she has a moment—some breathing space, lol—to practice. She takes one deep breath while counting to four. She wonders about how a person can do an action in a public space and yet be utterly invisible. She is holding at the top of her breath and counting to four again when she hears a shriek and a thump at the entrance. She glances at her watch. Friday 11:15. She thinks, *These people have nothing else to do than stick to a plan.* The shriek had come from the big Latino guy. He almost always does that when he hits the door. The others are in a clump around him, but the guy who shrieks is so tall that his voice carries across the store. The phone guy and his kid are checking out at Val's station, and the guy looks up from his call to see the source of the noise. That one shriek is all there is. The weird group slowly moves into the store. There are ten people and two handlers. People. Of course they're people. It's just that they look fuzzy around the edges, as if they haven't fully materialized after their interplanetary transport. Avery imagines that the group's van is like the Magic School Bus and comes from a different moment in history every Friday. No wonder they look so dazed in the fluorescent lights.

The group follows the same route through the store every week. As if the handlers don't have the authority to switch things up. To go down the central aisle with the housewares instead of going left through Apparel and Shoes first. The funky people are on autopilot. They shuffle their feet as if they're wearing slippers. Several of them wear Crocs, which might as well be slippers. It's usually quiet in here on a Friday morning, which is obviously why they come now. Tuesday mornings are even quieter, but Avery imagines that they save Target for Friday, for what? A reward? A threat? If you step out of line, no Target for you? These people do not look like they're having fun. The little group shambles out of Avery's line of sight. Avery checks out a few normal people. The odd folks should be coming around again for the third aisle. They walk up and down the main arteries of the store without stopping as a group, although there are stragglers and the occasional prison break when one of the people makes for the door. The handlers look young, but they take care of business when necessary. One thing about the helpers, they don't have their phones out. Avery sees the rectangles in their back pockets and admires their discipline.

Avery noticed this group when she first started working weekday mornings a year ago. She takes classes at the community college and figured out that she was better at focus in the afternoon, and mornings at Target are blissfully quiet. When she first saw them come in, they were like a single entity, a unit, a bunch of bananas, identifiable as individual bananas, but functionally defined as a single thing. A bunch. At first she didn't realize that they came every week at the same time. She felt dumb that it took her four weeks to figure that out. After that she looked out for them. She noticed that their arrival time did not vary by more than five minutes. It could be 11:14 or 11:18, but never 11:21. Somebody somewhere runs a tight ship. At first the clump of people was indistinguishable to Avery, but over the course of weeks she came to recognize a few. Sometimes she was doing checkout, sometimes putting back returns, but Friday chill gave her the space to observe. The disabled people were mostly the same from week to week. If someone acted up one Friday, they might not come the next week. The assistants wore the same T-shirt with the place's name on them, but they were not the same people every time. Avery doesn't think they make very much.

The tall Latino shrieker is a regular. Despite the outburst of noise when he enters, he is the most docile person Avery has ever seen. There is a young guy who repeats lines from videos over and over, sometimes as a droning white noise, sometimes high-pitched and anxious, but constant. Avery sees how that could get annoying over a whole day. There are only a few women who come. Women? Avery thinks of the mouse who is so withdrawn that she disappears in the group. She appears to be over twenty-one, but she is a child in all other ways. There is only one wheelchair in the group. Before this, Avery had automatically associated wheelchairs and disability. They all seem to have something terribly wrong with them, although Avery couldn't name it. She was just glad that it—at least this—wasn't her problem. They don't even go through her checkout stand because they never buy anything. That's what makes this weekly exercise so sad to Avery. There must be someone (the same person who keeps the trains running on time?) who thought these people needed an outing but didn't trust them to choose an item to buy or to handle money. That is a bad life assignment. Both sides of the equation.

Avery has just completed a transaction when the chunky group lurches around the corner in the direction of the exit. She glances at her watch. 11:46. Clockwork with a touch of wiggle room. Her shift is over at noon. She has Sociology at 2:00 and has time enough to finish the chapter if she stays on it. She wonders what separates herself from the people crawling into the white van parked in the red zone outside the door. She has a plan. That's the difference.

Before Avery even realizes it, a shriek near the door announces that Friday has come around again. Avery keeps her head down and focuses on pushing items across the glass eye at the end of the conveyer belt. Moms clog her station with under-$10 end-of-year teacher gifts. She glances up from a soap-and-lotion set and senses that she's missed her people altogether. Objectively she knows she should be pleased; it means the day is zooming by. She feels a palpable loss anyway. Her day will be less without them. Her time wavers.

The following Friday she is prepared. Avery checks her watch repeatedly. Around ten, she stops and feels silly. She wonders why she is so concerned with the people from the day care center. *What do you care?* She decides that the group has worked itself into her weekly routine and represents the end of her work week. Coincidence of work schedule. This is what she's thinking when the shriek happens near the door at— checks watch—11:16. Avery follows the group with her eyes as they begin their pointless perambulation. Is it her, or is the little group a little energized today? There is a bubble of fun hovering over them that Avery swears wasn't there before. Does she see it because there's something different in the group, or is her—Avery's—mood lighter? No, she's the same as she always is.

Avery watches the group as they come down the Housewares aisle. Behind the disabled people, she notices that the two aides in matching T-shirts are chatting. That's all. They're just shooting the breeze. Like she might talk with Val in the break room. It's a girl and a guy, no sexual energy, just co-workers chatting while performing their task of keeping the adults safe from themselves and each other. She also notices that the girl aide is new, new to Avery, anyway. The new girl is pretty in a college girl way. The guy aide is a little older, Hispanic, looks like he's at home with the job. The girl is doing all the talking. Avery knows this girl, her type. She's somebody's precious, has been persuaded that everything about her is worthwhile, that everyone is interested in what she has to say. Avery sees these girls at community college. The girls who didn't get into USC out of high school but will transfer when they get better grades. Avery hates these girls out of habit. This one, chatting up her co-worker, appears to be slumming it. Nobody does those health aide jobs if they could work retail. Avery looked it up once. Minimum wage, hard work in icky conditions. Target employees get a ten percent discount just for starters.

Avery watches out of the corner of her eye as the group makes the big turn in front of her station toward Personal Care, like an ocean liner changing direction in a rolling sea. The college girl in the ugly purple T-shirt sustains her spirited narration to her colleague, who keeps his wary eye on the disabled people in his care. Avery's attention is drawn back to the lady in front of her. The middle-aged white woman has followed Avery's glance and says, "Those poor people." Avery doesn't reply. She thinks about whether pity is the reaction she feels when she sees them. Curiosity is more like it. It's presumptuous to assume that they're miserable. College girl wears it all outside. Maybe the funky people keep it all in. Avery falls between, perhaps closer on the scale to the quiet ones. Avery completes the sale politely. The lady didn't mean to be offensive, although Avery is still nauseated by the arrogance of her pity.

Avery doesn't know what it's like to be disabled, but she knows about other things. She has a stepdad who doesn't like her very much and a mom too weak to stand up for her. He wants Avery out of the house, which makes her want it, too. Her natural lack of initiative has slowed the process. The atmosphere at home is motivating, and she feels like she might be able to get it together this year.

*

It's full-on summer and Avery's once-quiet weekday mornings are noisy with moms and kids buying pool noodles and stuff for camp and summer school. There are other day camps that make field trips out of going to Target. Mr. Target ought to charge admission. Her Friday regulars get lost in the summer shuffle. Avery loses track of them for a couple of weeks. She thinks a lot about what to do in the fall. She has spent four years slogging through general studies stuff at the community college one or two classes at a time. As long as she's enrolled and showing up, Avery feels like she's working toward a future. She can't see the direction yet, still. She has mastered the world of retail. It's time to saddle up and hit the trail.

During her break, Avery sits at a round red table outside and makes a list of all the classes she enjoyed at college. It is surprisingly long. Every class annoyed her with deadlines and reading, and most professors are boring. But in hindsight, she got a lot out of her psychology class and she legit liked being in the anthropology lab with all the bones and skulls. What corresponds with a job she could work toward? She notices a white passenger van pulling up in front of the store to let out its passengers. Avery perks up to see that it's her friends, the disabled people. She notices the Upward Bound logo on the side of the van. The manly Hispanic aide gets out of the van so smartly that Avery wonders why he doesn't have a more professional kind of job. She sees her red T-shirt and her list of classes. Easier said than done.

Avery never thought about what it took to get the funky people to the store. Watching the slow-motion routine is painful. Most of them can get out on their own. The girl aide oversees their exiting and keeps them in one place while the guy deals with the wheelchair. What an ordeal, the whole thing. It's amazing they ever leave their place. Avery would just stay home. Her break ends before the group is ready to enter the store. The guy has to park the van. Avery passes as close to the group as she's ever been. She tries to smile in a friendly way but feels awkward. She ducks her head and gets her first good look at the person in the wheelchair. It's a young man, about twenty-five or so. He is so good-looking that Avery is stunned for a moment. Her focus pulls back and she sees how very disabled he is. His face is exquisite, though. It's a disconcerting sight. She sidles past the group as discreetly as possible. She slips her list into her back pocket and goes back to work.

Avery dances a little behind her checkout stand to the Muzak. The group is in the store but out of her vision. Avery wonders about the wheelchair guy, about what's wrong with him, who takes care of him when he's not at the place. What kind of therapist deals with someone like that? She has a vision of herself, not in a red T-shirt and black pants, but in a blue scrubs outfit. She is helping a disabled man walk along parallel handlebars, like in those Wounded Warrior commercials. Avery can see herself in a job like that. Nothing mental or psychological, but she could tend to broken bodies. She never had a desire to be a nurse. Too much walking and pressure. But a crippled person's therapist? It felt like something she could accomplish. A job she could make money at where she could help people. Avery isn't sure what kind of therapy she's thinking of. Occupational or physical? She has seen both in the college course listings. She could talk to someone in the advising office. Avery is consumed by these ideas rushing through her head. She transacts her tasks on autopilot.

Avery's busy brain is halted in midflight. A flash of blond and chrome lights up an inner aisle. Office Supplies. The halo of light erupts above the shelving and shoots out into the main aisle toward Party Supplies. She hears giggling and rubber treads in motion. The sound and activity recede momentarily. She can't imagine a reasonable explanation for the phenomenon. Suddenly the blond chrome creature streaks across the area in front of checkout. Avery, astonished, recognizes college girl aide as she rides on the back of movie star's wheelchair.

They have gotten up a good head of steam coming around the corner from Women's Apparel. College girl is laughing, throat forward, but makes less sound than it looks like she's making. The man/boy in the wheelchair is scrunched up almost in a ball, with his head back and his mouth gaping open. It looks terrifying to Avery at first, like he's being horribly hurt, but she realizes that the guy is loving it. Joy looks like agony on that guy.

Avery is stopped in her tracks. She reminds herself to close her mouth, which had fallen open in wonderment. Her head and gaze follow the pair as they streak across the floor at an unsafe rate of speed. The girl controls the flying wheelchair surprisingly well, and she takes the turn toward Pet Care and Toys without going up on two wheels. It seems gravity- and physics-defying, like a cartoon where the usual rules are shattered. The vision disappears from her field as abruptly as it came, leaving behind a faint streak of loss. The area in front of her stand is quiet and tawdry. The goods are cheap. The candy has no sustenance. The floor is scuffed in parallel lines.

Avery feels her lungs empty as she turns to process the purchases of an older man buying Depends and melatonin. She feels betrayed. College girl aide and her energy have put the disabled people—Avery's disabled people, as she thinks of them—out of her reach. That bubbly thing that some girls do makes Avery feel invisible. She doesn't have the gene. The group from the place was like a full-length mirror from aisle 16 for Avery. She recognized a formless flatness about them. College girl sprinkles her fairy dust on them and suddenly they are fun? Avery badly wants to resent college girl for her privileged personality. But she thinks about wheelchair guy. He deserves a little amusement in his life.

Avery's thoughts are interrupted when college girl, wheelchair guy, and tall Latino shrieker come moving slowly around the corner where the chrome chair had made the harrowing turn a few minutes ago. College girl had to wrangle a straggler and she took wheelchair guy on a joyride to get the job done. Now she has collected her wanderer and they slowly make their way back to the unseen others. The three of them make a little family. Avery notices that the girl is pushing the chair with one hand only. Her other hand, as Avery can see as they slowly turn down the central aisle, is resting lightly on the back of the big Latino's arm. The gesture is so tender that Avery's heart catches. The flibberty girl has a sweet soul. *Goddammit,* thinks Avery, *I'd rather she was shallow.* It would conform to her world construct that the lucky can't also be good.

It takes the purifying fire of hard struggle to make the hero. This is what Avery's been banking on. That her journey has more value because it's not a straight path. Adversity as an incentive for soul building. For the first time, Avery wants to have gone away to school. The evidence that college girl has a soul makes Avery wonder if there is something special delivered in a class you have to go away to take. Lessons you don't get if your travel to campus is under five miles from your high school. Whatever, ship has sailed. Avery smiles as sincerely as she can as she hands the old man his diapers in an expensive plastic bag that she feels bad charging him for. He would have gotten it for free back in the days before he needed diapers. Every human struggles with something. Incontinence has got to be a burden.

Avery watches over a customer's shoulder as the Upward Bound group slumps toward the door. College girl is smiling and repeating back the movie line that video guy is stuck on. She's matching his high pitch and Avery can hear them from a distance. College girl doesn't care, isn't embarrassed. Video guy is gratified. Avery wonders if college girl is leaving soon; it's August. She will leave a hole in the Friday group. Avery tries to picture herself in college girl's place.

August starts moving fast. Avery's school starts before Labor Day and she's excited, which is weird. She's been talking to a counselor in the advising office at the community college, a place where Avery has always felt anonymous. She told the woman about wheelchair guy and the disabled group and asked how you become one of those therapists. The lady took an interest. There are several paths to becoming an occupational or physical therapist, but that comes after regular college. Avery figures it out over breaks at work, huddling over her phone and clicking on every academic program the place offers. She's under the red umbrella in front of the store when she presses the Register button for fall. She needs a health sciences class and an education class and she can graduate in winter and get her applications in for transfer. The advisor lady seemed sure that Avery would get into a state school with financial aid. Maybe she could go for a reach school, see what happens.

Avery is looking over her class schedule when she realizes that the health sciences class is on Friday mornings, the only time it's offered. She'll have to talk to Fenicia about adjusting her work schedule for this quarter. It occurs to Avery that not working on Fridays means not seeing her people. She has a thought: If that class has a research paper or something, maybe she could do hers on the place, on Upward Bound. She drove past it on her way to work this morning. She was curious about where her people are when they're not at Target. The building was brown and sad looking. No wonder college girl was so affable in the store. She was just glad to be out of there. It was the color of poop. Avery looks at the registration confirmation.

It's the third Friday of August. Avery acts like it's no big deal to switch her Friday shifts to afternoons for fall. This is her last Friday morning, at least for now. She's aware, completely aware, that her obsession with the people is weird. It's probably because her job has gotten a little boring. Avery used to make the time pass by watching and judging the customers. But people turn out to be stupid in similar ways, in a limited number of similar ways. She's seen it play out a million times by now and it's not entertaining her the way it used to.

Avery finishes her tea brought from home, takes one last look at the class schedule that starts Tuesday, and gets up from the picnic table. Her spirits are elevated when she sees the white van pulling into the parking lot. She takes her time putting her things together so she can watch them get out. The first thing she notices is that someone else is driving. The cute, competent Hispanic guy isn't here today. She wonders about him, maybe she has a little crush on him and always hoped he'd notice her. Too late now. Too many missed opportunities in her life, and she makes a promise to herself to seize them from now on. She watches the disembarkation process out of the corner of her eye. It's more awkward without the cool guy, slow and sad somehow, like he was the one with the world on his shoulders. She turns and goes back into the store. Fenicia must wonder where she is by now.

Acting like it's a regular Friday, Avery takes the little "Closed, Please Use Next Register" sign off the conveyor belt but doesn't look up as the goods are placed in front of her.

THE ELOPER
PART II

One day not long ago, Jorge showed up in obvious distress. He arrives every morning on a short bus, so there was no family member who could brief the staff on what might have precipitated this unusual level of agitation. In case you're curious, my mother never allowed them to transport me on the short bus, even though it's a funded service. She always said it was about keeping me safe, but I also think it was about maintaining dignity. The fact that "short bus" is synonymous with "retarded" is part of it. But it is also a great challenge to be stuck in a small space filled with autistic adults who are rocking, flapping, and vocalizing. Even if I am one of them. Most Upward Bound families took advantage of the bus.

No one could say why Jorge was upset that day. I noticed that he was burning holes in the closet door with his lidded eyes since breakfast. A lot of adults with autism like toys that you're used to seeing in a preschooler's toy chest. I am pretty subtle about it, but there might be a bin or three of Thomas the Tank

Engine and his friends in my room at home. So I had an understanding of why Jorge was clawing at the locked closet door that morning. He was in a terrible mood for whatever reason, and he really needed some quality time with Mr. Potato Head.

Carlos saw Jorge struggling and came over to help. He knew Jorge well enough to understand his objective. He's well aware of the rule against opening the Pandora's box of the toy closet when it's not the scheduled activity, but Carlos could see that this was becoming an emergency. He pulled out his ring of keys, and the clinking sound alerted other inmates. An excited little crowd gathered around him. Carlos was trying to tell the others that he was just getting a Potato Head for Jorge. But everybody had a comfort item in that closet. Carlos opened the door just a crack and the others started to push in with anxious arms. Jorge smelled a threat. Moving at the speed of light, he yanked the special spud off the shelf and was out the rec room door before Carlos could register it. Another short bus had arrived and the door to the outside was propped open for a wheelchair. As big as he was, Jorge slipped through the gauntlet and was down the sidewalk in a stealthy dash. I followed to see what would happen. I wanted to be a human breadcrumb for Carlos to follow. He was still extricating himself from the scrum of toy grabbers. Finally Carlos rushed past me and out the door, but Jorge was already crossing the street.

Jorge didn't go far; he wasn't running away. He just needed some space and privacy to commune with Potato Head. He dodged oncoming cars to reach the little park. A passing police car had to slam on its brakes to avoid hitting Jorge. On the other side, he sat on a parking berm and held on tight to the toy. Carlos was on the other side of the road and watched as the police car turned around and faced Jorge in the park's parking lot. The police got out of their car and were asking questions of Jorge. Jorge was rocking back and forth, clutching the toy to his belly and emitting a disturbing shriek. Carlos was waiting for cars to pass before he could dash across to the park. He could see that the cops had their hands poised over their guns and started yelling at them to back off as he ran across the road. The cops were barking out orders at Jorge, which only escalated Jorge's behavior. Jorge suddenly lifted up his hands to cover his ears, Potato Head still tightly gripped. Only god knows why the younger cop panicked at this sight. What harm did he think Jorge was going to do with a plastic tuber? The cop drew his gun and fired. Carlos had just moved in to comfort Jorge. The bullet hit Carlos in the abdomen. Another bullet wound up in a play structure behind them.

Dave and other staffers were running toward the park. I noticed that Mariana, the secretary, was running fastest, a weird look on her face. The cop who had fired stared blankly at his work, frozen in place. The cop who hadn't fired called for an ambulance. Carlos lay bleeding in the parking lot. A small pool of blood gathered beneath him. Jorge was flailing. He never stopped vocalizing as he stood and jumped and flapped his hands. Potato Head flew out of his grasp and fell somewhere behind him, unable to placate any longer.

Things moved quickly at that point. The ambulance arrived and took Carlos away. Mariana hovered and wept, and they let her go with him in the ambulance. We later learned that he passed away en route to the hospital. Despite Dave's assurances that Jorge was not a psycho, just autistic, the police took him on a 5150, a seventy-two-hour psychiatric hold. If you ask me, the trigger-happy cop deserved a trip to the loony bin more than Jorge.

When my mom heard about the shooting, she rushed over to pick me up. She hustled me out of the building in the chaos, not even bothering to sign me out. My mom kept saying:

"Never. You'll never have to go back there. I swear." This was one of those times when all that could soothe me was an enveloping bear hug from Dad. Mom was too skinny for the job. When we got home, I retreated behind my noisy bank of video screens. *Toy Story 3* was on the biggest one. The scene in the dump's incinerator on repeat. My mom came in. The ominous music alarmed her. I made no indication that the day's events had disturbed me. She's not an idiot. She led me to our workroom and held up the letter board.

"Tell me," she said.

I pointed, "J O R G E W H A T H A P P E N S T O H I M."

"Honey, I don't know. I can call Dave tomorrow. But even if he knows, they probably won't let him say. Privacy rules and all that."

She called Upward Bound in the morning but learned nothing. She went online. That may have been a mistake. Trolls and assholes placed the blame on Jorge, claiming he was the reason that Carlos was in the line of fire. Freaks like Jorge shouldn't be allowed near our homes or in our parks. People like Jorge should be shipped off to an institution where they can't bother the rest of us. Of course, the language they used on Twitter was not so civilized. I screamed at my screens all day.

We got through those first few days, but I'm not sure how. I was basically numb. It hadn't been so long since we lost my dad, so I wasn't ready for another blow. I stayed on my noisy screens and Mom sat at her sewing machine with *Top Chef* reruns playing bingily on the TV. It's tough when your heart is trying to block the past, the present, and the future. At least one of those ought to be tolerable. A week after the event, Mom got an email from Upward Bound saying that there was to be a memorial service for Carlos the following Friday. I felt a great and unexpected relief from this news. I hadn't realized how unsettled I was, not just by the shooting, but also by the abrupt, unresolved way I had ended that brief, rotten chapter of my life. I am grateful to people like Darla, Andy, and Carlos for seeing me, and in hindsight I think I formed a few actual friendships. I found that I wanted to say goodbye to Drew and Emma and Tom. I wanted to say goodbye to Dave, even though . . . even though.

The memorial gave us a reason to wake up a little. I needed something to wear. I would have worn something of my dad's, but his funeral-appropriate clothes were old and dusty, and they didn't fit. He was more of a sweatpants guy. I have a uniform that I'm comfortable with: basketball shorts, a Pixar T-shirt, and Crocs. No buttons, no zippers. No tags on anything. Tags feel like a cactus next to my skin. I have been wearing this since I was in preschool. I have one soft polo shirt that I can wear to a nice place, but I had to do better than that for Carlos. Mom had the black dress she had worn to Dad's funeral, so she was set. I actually wore the lonely polo shirt for Dad's service, because there was only so much I could handle that day. Dad would have wanted me to be comfortable. But I wanted to show Carlos respect, and I wanted to look like an adult to bid farewell to Upward Bound.

Mom and I went to the mall. I like the mall, even though it's obviously overstimulating. The lights and people and the thrum of fluorescent electricity that undergirds the floors and stores give my brain a bright holiday. Of course, I am rarely required to deal with clothing purchases. Ninety-nine percent of my wardrobe is purchased online. But once every couple of years I have to try on and buy something fancy, something typical people wear without thinking about it. Mom has figured out how to do this in a way that limits my agony. This time, she was particularly mindful as to how far she could push me. We went into the least-swanky department store and she sat me in a chair with my iPad and phone. My tolerance issues are coupled with my weird body to make finding a nice pair of well-fitting pants a virtual impossibility. Mom went to the sale rack and quickly came back with three pants possibilities. I tried them on, with Mom commandeering the hooks and zipper. The second pair worked pretty well, so we stopped there. She also pulled two sport coats, but they were too expensive, even on the sale rack. She announced that one of Dad's jackets would be okay after all. We managed to find a pair of pull-on shoes that were reasonably comfortable, although they were hardly Crocs. Once these tasks were performed, we walked through the LEGO store and ate Panda Express in the food court. By the time we got back to Mom's car, I was feeling okay again.

We woke up Friday morning and went through the motions of our usual routine. Sometimes a routine can be a lifeline. The air in our house was filled with tension and waiting for the clock to tick down another minute. Finally it was time to get dressed. Lousy fine motor skills and a lack of experience with little shirt buttons meant that Mom had to help me. As if I really were the child that Upward Bound treated me as. I really don't like this adult-neurotypical costume. We almost had a problem when Mom had to tie Dad's twenty-year-old tie around my neck. She didn't know how. Dad did it for me before. We looked it up on YouTube. It almost made us late.

The memorial was held in a big Catholic church. I had only thought of Carlos as belonging to Upward Bound, so it was enlightening to see how many other moving parts his life had. He obviously came from a large Latino family. I spotted Mariana in the center of a group of aunties and cousins. It had never dawned on me before, but I suddenly realized that Carlos and Mariana were brother and sister. What must that day in the parking lot have been like for her? I was glad she was in the ambulance at least, so someone was with him who loved him. I saw a diverse group of young people consoling each other. I imagined them to be Carlos's kayak friends. If only they knew how often I had daydreamed about being one of them.

Mom and I just sort of stood there. People are generally disinclined to approach me, especially people who see my disability and are perplexed. I get it. It's awkward to talk to someone who can't talk back, who makes strange noises with their fingers in their ears. No eye contact. Some therapists make a big deal about eye contact, as if, were I to meet this elusive goal, I would make friends and blend into typical society. As we nonspeakers like to say (contradiction intended), I can either look at you or listen to you. Choose one. Your face in motion is so bright, so stimulating, so loud and beautiful, that my senses are overwhelmed. I must look away to focus on what you're saying. Typical people always get this wrong. So Mom and I are used to hovering on the periphery of a crowd. We could see Dave. He's tall. Mom tried getting his attention to say hello, but he seemed determined not to see us. As if my leaving at that terrible time was a personal betrayal to him. Even though I never really liked Dave, his coldness hurt. Mom and I cut our losses and went into the church.

I am a back-row sitter from way back. I don't like for anyone to sit behind me—I feel like they're counting my tics. I like having a little distance between the central action and me. It lessens the sensory assault of the film, the speaker, or the entertainer. Mom says that she's the opposite. She loves the front row for its immersive properties. One of the countless personal preferences she sacrifices for my sake. We take seats in the back pew of the immense church. I watch people come in, although it looks like I'm looking at a muted video on my iPad. Peripheral vision is my strongest visual channel. It's like a superpower that keeps others from knowing that you're spying on them. I witnessed the family enter in sad, angry clumps. Carlos was the victim of a wrongful police shooting, not because he was brown, but because they were aiming at the autistic guy and missed. There were so many layers of wrong here that my brain hurt. Carlos was the best thing about Upward Bound. He treated us with respect, like we were human beings, like our differences were not a choice. I could see in the way that family members looked at me and talked among themselves that a big portion of blame for Carlos's death was being leveled at Upward Bound and, by extension, clients like me. I thought about Jorge, but I didn't see him. Of course he's not here. I doubt he had any staff or family who could have brought him. His family might not even know what Carlos meant to Jorge. While I wished Jorge could be here, I could fully grasp that his presence would have caused distress for Carlos's family. The weight of the world's pain was making it hard for me to breathe.

A pipe organ began to play a hymn. I didn't recognize it, but I'd only been in a church a couple of times. My mom tried to take me to the children's program at a progressive church when I was little, but my wild behaviors were too much even for those well-intended liberal ladies. Once a church rejects you, for whatever reason, it's hard to view Jesus as a source of salvation. So I don't know many hymns. I listened to the pounding, thunderous organ and I thought of how dissonant the bombast was in relation to Carlos. He was quiet and sweet and thoughtful, the opposite in every way from this bullying sound, intended apparently to coerce you by force into following Jesus. The organ stopped. Everyone stood up and sat down a few times. I wasn't interested in the words being said. I couldn't really understand them in the cavernous building. There was no casket in the front, as Mom had said there might be. Maybe the police still had his body. I have grown up with a healthy skepticism about institutions that have failed me. Education, conventional medicine, psychiatry, religion, Upward Bound. I'm not skeptical about police anymore. I am legitimately terrified that someday a trigger-happy officer will mistake my unusual behaviors for a threat to society and mow me down, too.

There was a big poster-sized picture of Carlos propped on an easel down front. It was an old picture, maybe even his high school graduation portrait. What was funny was that Carlos looked like an arrogant troublemaker in the picture. His hair was long and his chin pointed in the air. The priest in front was finally talking about Carlos instead of god. It sounded like the priest had known Carlos a long time and that he was very sad. Apparently Carlos was a little wild when he was a kid. His dad had left their family and the mom had to work two jobs. Older sister Mariana did her best to take care of him. Mariana went to college and got the job at Upward Bound. When Carlos was in some real trouble after high school, Mariana got him a job there. No one thought it would work. I heard Dave in the crowd let out a little snort-laugh as if to tell everyone, "Yeah, I was there, I turned Carlos around." Carlos did turn his life around, although I doubt that Dave had much to do with it. Carlos had found himself in Jorge and Drew and Emma and me. His calm center was located in our dysregulated brains. Yin and yang. Carlos was happy with us. I don't know that the priest said all that, but it was what I was thinking while he spoke.

The organ thundered again and a group of family members led the way out. Women clutched each other while the men tried to look stoic. Mom and I waited to leave. I kept looking for familiar faces to pass, but Dave and Mariana were it. That made sense, I guess. Most Upward Bound parents would be working, and group home caregivers don't take clients to something like this. I think it's something else, too. The inmates of Upward Bound were not adequately capable of communicating how important Carlos was to them, to the people who could have facilitated getting them to the service. I felt like I was representing all of us. I thought I had wanted some sort of farewell or resolution, but maybe the fact that I was here and they were not was the point. I was able to call my own shots, or point at them anyway. That set me apart. I couldn't belong to this club of silence, I refused, but I could tell stories from behind the front lines.

There was a reception in the church hall, but we didn't stay long. Mom said something nice to Mariana. She is always so sweet and calm in her office—a reason I should have guessed she and Carlos were related—that it was gutting to see her so sad. After Mom gave her a little side hug, Mariana looked right at me and said, "Carlos always liked you, Walter. He mentioned that he was curious about your typing. We're going to miss you." I was stunned. I felt special, the good kind of special.

Mom said, "What do you say, Walter?" This prompt usually means that I am supposed to say, "Thank you," so I did. Sometimes this comes out as "Happy birthday" or "It's time to go," so I was glad I nailed it this time.

Dave was still avoiding us. I grabbed four sugar cookies before Mom stopped me. They didn't have Coke, which was disappointing. Coke can help any awkward situation. Just then I saw Dave hovering over Mom's head at the dessert table. He looked down and his face showed surprise, as if he had just now noticed that we were there. I wasn't buying it, of course. I think that he didn't know anyone else, either, and that it was less awkward to talk to us than to keep ignoring us.

"Well," he said, "fancy seeing you here."

Good thing I don't have good fine motor control or I would have been rolling my eyes. Mom to the rescue yet again.

"Yes, Walter wanted to pay his respects."

"I wish that more of the Upward Bound folks could be here, but it's a workday and there are clients to care for." There was an unspoken jab at us. "I assume that Walter isn't coming back."

"No, he's been through a lot lately and we're going to take some time to figure things out."

"I have some paperwork for you to sign, and you should check the Lost and Found box."

"Okay, we'll come in this week and deal with that. What do you say, Walter?"

My mind raced to summon the correct script for the moment. "Thank you" was the best response I could summon, but I'm not sure it was right.

I finally made it clear that it was time to go. Mom told me to turn my voice down as we moved to the exit as discreetly as possible. We got home and I quickly changed out of the restrictive clothes. Time took on a slow, unreal quality. Videos occupied my hours but not my mind. Mom was absent-minded. She forgot how much reading out loud helped soothe my agitation. I went to great loud lengths to remind her.

We went to Upward Bound on Monday. My stomach clenched when we pulled up. I sat in the lobby with Edith while Mom dealt with the paperwork. Mariana was still out, so Dave had to do the copying and whatnot. There was nothing of mine in the Lost and Found box. I knew that. When Mom was done, we walked into the rec room. It was snack time. I looked around the familiar room and faces. I smelled the smells. They were alien to me already. The atmosphere was like a nursing home, as if the building were reverting to its original purpose. As if the forest were reclaiming the clearing after the cabin burned down. I was finally able to focus on the faces huddled over the plastic tables. I saw Emma, her nice face frozen in neutral, her sharp eyes darting under dull lids. There was Drew, prattling on, repeating my birth date without mentioning my name. A girl staffer whose name I didn't know was helping Tom eat his snack, but she was distracted and wasn't really looking at him. I remembered Ann and it struck me how much Tom must miss her. At the end of the table, hunched over so far that you could hardly see his face, was Jorge. He wasn't eating—he wasn't really there. There was an empty seat across from him. I wanted to go sit there, but as usual my body refused to initiate the action. Mom saw the seat, too, and led me over to it. In my heart I told him all sorts of supportive words. I hope his heart heard them, although I don't know. Only Carlos could have helped him. I sat there for a while. Andy gave me a little bowl of cheese puffs, generic. Mom chatted with staffers and also spent a few moments with Tom. She put her arm around Jorge and whispered something in his ear. He didn't look up at her, but his big body leaned just slightly toward her. For Jorge, that was a hug. Mom gestured for me to get up. We stood in front of the people I'd been spending my days with for months. Almost no one looked up at me, but I knew that they had no more control over their bodies than I did.

Mom nudged me. "What do you say, Walter?"

I've got a script for this. I got it off of a *Blue's Clues* episode and I am capable of summoning it at will:

"Goodbye, everyone!" I called out in my best upbeat Steve voice. I even incorporated a cheery wave.

The only client to say bye back was Drew, but he said it several times. Andy and the staffers called out good wishes. Nothing to do but leave. So we did.

*

That part of our lives was done, and there was no chapter outline for what happens afterward.

The first few weeks we treated ourselves to a staycation. We did the things I enjoyed when I was younger. We went to the aquarium, the science museum, the mall, and the movies. We ran out of ideas (my list of preferred activities is short), so we picked out a Dickens novel—*Bleak House,* why not indulge—and Mom read out loud a couple hours a day. I did a jigsaw puzzle. I came upon Mom squinting at the computer.

"I think I can get paid for being your caregiver," she said.

Her internet search generated numerous interviews with social workers, home visits from officers of the court, and paperwork. At the end of it all, she was officially a service provider and I was receiving SSI. We did the math. This new support was about equal to what Mom had been making at the hospital job. Neither of us liked being dependent on public money, but we were probably what the system had in mind when they instituted such assistance. Mom looked at our situation. Dad had always done the bills. Mom told me that if we moved into a smaller place, we could probably get by. This was a hard pill to swallow. This was Dad's dream house. But he wouldn't want Mom working and me in day care just to stay here. We put the house on the market and it sold quickly. Our lives were subsumed with house hunting and a million moving boxes. Mom had to be ruthless about getting rid of stuff. This meant tossing Dad's ridiculous collections of bobbleheads, mini helmets, and VHS cassettes. She broke down just a couple of times, like when she put the dusty skateboard signed by Tony Hawk in the donate pile. She had teased him a million times about the dubious value of this precious artifact. We bought a townhouse in a quiet area. We moved. The less said about that wretched day the better.

The need for a new routine was crushing my brain. My mother was made painfully aware of this by my loud, uncontrollable scripting.

"You wanna pack the box?"

"You wanna get on the truck?"

The moving truck was long gone. We had already unpacked the boxes and put everything away. I knew we were not going anywhere, that we were where we were supposed to be. I was mourning my old life patterns, and repeating the impossible gave me a perverse comfort. The problem for Mom was that I repeated those obsolete scripted phrases about 150,000 times a day in an anxious high-pitched voice.

Mostly to shut me up and to give our lives some order, Mom instituted a daily schedule of reading. We finished *Bleak House* and moved on to *War and Peace*. That may sound like a joke, but we had time and nothing better to do with it. To break up the monotony of the reading, Mom had me do a couple of twenty-minute writing sessions per day.

"Write me something about your dad," she said. "It will be nice to have your memories so we can look back on them."

So I wrote reminiscences about how he made bad jokes, how loudly he talked on the phone, how I could do no wrong in his eyes. After that, I wrote some memories about Carlos, about his love of the outdoors and how cool he was to the clients at Upward Bound. I also wrote about Jorge, imagining how it must have felt to be him on the day that Carlos was shot. I pondered how Jorge was doing without him. I even wrote a speculative bit about how Jorge and I were friends for real.

Suddenly Mom and I had a new routine that filled our days with work that might not be literally productive but still felt meaningful. In the breaks between our sessions of reading and writing, Mom did chores or her craft projects. She enjoyed quilting. It took her out of her responsibilities, and it was all hers. She was currently working on a quilt made from Dad's favorite old sports team T-shirts. I vegged out on my video screens. I could see us going on like this. We developed two possible future plans: for me to transfer to a university and finish a bachelor's degree, or just keep writing and see what happens. Either sounded good to me. I was in no hurry. The days took care of themselves. The only thing missing from our benign stasis was a guy poking his nudgy head in the door. Mom and I were not like Carlos and Jorge. We were not simply content without our third leg. I had always thought of us three as a unit. Now I am seeing that Mom and Dad were a unit before I ever came along. She is missing an entire half of herself. I can't fill that space, but I'm not going anywhere.

ACKNOWLEDGMENTS

Annie Woods and Kyle Brown are the best sisters a guy like me could have. They sent me on my way. They also gave me two awesome brothers, Matt Garrett and Travis Libin. Many thanks to the people who helped me crawl out of the pit of ignorance and isolation: Soma Mukhopadhyay, Katie Anawalt, Darlene Hanson, Peggy Schaefer, Cheryl Kemery, Sal Battaglia, Anne Chaney, Naomi Montgomery, Isalia Zumaya, and many others. Much gratitude to Mona Simpson, who showed me what writers do. Rivka Galchen, you made me better when I felt weak and powerless. Ben Marcus and Sam Lipsyte both cheered me up and cheered me on. Paul Beatty opened a new window. Sarah Chalfant of the Wylie Agency believed in me, and David Ebershoff at Hogarth took me to a whole new world of acceptance. I also want to call out to the world of nonspeakers and their caregivers. We are in camaraderie together.